BITTER INHERITANCE

I0675727

Dr. Mildred Dumàs

Professional Publishing House   California

Published and Distributed by
Professional Publishing House
1425 W. Manchester Ave., Suite B
Los Angeles, California 90047
www.professionalpublishinghouse.com
Drrosie@aol.com
(323) 750-3592

Cover design by George Hooks
Second Edition
First printing second edition June, 2011
ISBN: 978-0-983-4444-2-8
10987654321

BITTER INHERITANCE

Dr. Mildred Dumàs

Other Works by Dr. Mildred Dumàs

Books

FACADES
SEASON OF TEARS

Most Popular Plays
(Entire list is too numerous to name)

THE POWER OF MY WILL
(Drama)

UNCLE RUFUS I AND II
(Mystery Comedies)

LOOKING FOR A MAN
(With Sylvia Roberts)
(Dramatic Comedy)

MY BROTHERS' BLOOD
(With Ernestine Harbour)
(Drama)

WHEN THE PAST COMES BACK…
(Drama)

THE GRIEVING WIDOWS' AUXILIARY
(Comedy)

A GATHERING OF FIRST LADIES
(Historical Drama)

Acknowledgements

First, I would like to thank God for giving me a creative mind and the opportunity to use it to entertain, inform, enlighten, and educate others with my various writings.

Special thanks to Rochelle Williams and Dr. Elizabeth Marshall for all they have done to help move my writing career along: productions of many of my plays—and a book signing (hosted by Rochelle) for the first edition of this book.

Thanks to other friends and family members for hosting book signings of the first edition, also: Mr. and Mrs. Gregg Johnson; Catherine Dumas-St. Julian; my sister and brother-in-law, Mr. and Mrs. Gerold McGraw; and Linda Hughes.

To the book clubs that hosted book signings: The Hyde Park/Mariam Matthews Library Book Club, The Baldwin Hills Oasis Book Club, and The Antelope Valley African American Book Club—I am so grateful.

To Megan Willingham—for having me on her radio show to promote the first edition of this book and a second time to promote this edition and the upcoming movie—I am eternally grateful.

I am deeply indebted to friends and colleagues who have supported me throughout the years by coming to my play productions and book signings. To Norma Bellmar, who always brings others with her, my gratitude has no bounds.

To my family members who have supported me throughout all of my endeavors, thanks so much. To my two sisters, Ethel and Annie, who will hop on a plane in a minute to be with me at my openings be it a play, book signing... whatever is taking place; your support means the world to me.

Sincere thanks to George Hooks for designing the magnificent cover for this novel. You're the best.

And, finally, I would like to thank Dr. Rosie Milligan and her staff for their tireless efforts in helping me get this book in order for its Second Edition.

I love you all. God bless!

BITTER INHERITANCE

CHAPTER 1

"I'm glad he's dead! Do you hear me, Mother? I'm glad!"

Sonya had come into her mother's room immediately after they arrived home from the funeral. Claire remembered the hatred that emanated from her daughter's face. As if it had been etched there, she had thought.

Sonya's angry words still rang in her mother's ears. Claire had slapped her—the first time she had ever raised her hand to the girl.

Too late...much too late, Claire thought.

Claire Gene Colby stood over the grave dressed in all black. She wore a dress of simple lines, leather gloves that met the long sleeves of the dress at her wrists, a wide-brimmed hat that sat regally on her head, and a pair of alligator pumps that concealed her feet—all as black as the night that surrounded her, enhanced by the dark clouds that hung overhead threatening rain. All as black as her soul.

"Oh, William, I miss you so much." Claire's voice quivered, and tears coursed down her face. The expensive dress hung loosely on her emaciated frame. She had not eaten properly for a long time, not since William's affair with the other woman had begun, and especially since his death.

Before William died, Claire had thought, or rather hoped, there was a chance. He had loved her once. She could not believe their time together was gone. In spite of all that had happened, she continued to hope. She kept up her appearance, forced herself to eat and go through the motions of living for the few times she did see him. But now... She still loved him, but now she knew it was over. Forever. She had finally been forced to let go.

Death could be so cruel at times. Then, again, it could bring such sweet relief. Claire felt dead inside, as if her life had ended with his. Maybe it should have.

Her knees began to shake as she slowly knelt beside the grave. Her hands trembled as she reached out to place a single red rose beside the tombstone.

He had loved red roses. It had been their favorite flower. She picked them from the rose garden when they were in bloom. She put them on the dining table, in the foyer, out on the terrace where they had often dined together, and in their bedroom. During the winter, she had them delivered from the florist. They had filled the church at their wedding. *So many years ago*, she thought.

The first bolt of lightning flashed, and Claire looked at the writing on the marble slab that was momentarily illuminated.

WILLIAM ELLIS COLBY

1946-2011

"My dear, beloved husband," she whispered as sobs shook her body. She had wanted to put the inscription on William's tombstone, but Sonya had opposed the idea so vehemently. She would never forget that day or the look in her daughter's eyes.

"Fool!" the girl had screamed. "You're a blind, ignorant fool, Mother!"

The clouds opened up, and the rain began to pour. The figure that knelt at the grave did not seem to notice. Her hands embraced the tombstone, her head resting on the cold piece of marble. Her eyes were closed as if to shut out the rain, the world about her, all the people who lay in their cold beds around her—except the man in the grave beneath her. She wanted to see him, to will him to come to her, to tell her he had been wrong, that he had loved her until death—as he had promised—and that the other woman had meant nothing to him. If she could only hear his voice again, feel his touch.

Claire thought of times past when they had strolled hand-in-hand to the park; to church; to a restaurant where they had basked in each other over a succulent meal; to the theatre that they had both loved so much; to dances—many of them—where they had held each other, where their bodies had touched, swayed together as the melodious sounds engulfed them. William had been a good dancer. Following him was so easy. He just seemed to glide over the floor, and she went right along, following his lead. She had enjoyed her husband so much.

Claire wondered if William had danced with her, the other woman. How she had felt in the folds of his arms. If the woman had loved and appreciated him as much as she. Claire could not imagine how that could have been possible. No woman could have loved William the way she had—still did.

Death was only a temporary parting of the ways.

"You were my whole life, William," she sobbed. "I don't want to go on without you. I can't. You were mine. Mine, not hers. You belonged to me."

Claire felt strong hands tugging at her arms, pulling her to her feet.

"It's time to go, Mrs. Colby." Harry's voice, soft and caring, was close to her ear.

Claire trembled as she stood and allowed herself to be propelled toward the car. The urgency in her chauffeur's grip told her that they should hurry, but she could not make herself do so. Her William was there in the cold, wet, ground all alone. He never liked the rain. She wanted to stay with him, to comfort him, but she knew she had to go. She would not hurry, though. That would not be proper.

When Claire and Harry reached the car, they were both drenched. Harry yanked the back door open. Claire could feel his annoyance with her as he helped her into the back seat. The door slammed, and he hurried around to the driver's side.

10

"The old bat's crazy," he muttered to himself. He got into the limousine and drove away just as another bolt of lightning flashed. The entire cemetery was illuminated for a few seconds. A loud blast of thunder followed. Harry shivered. He did not like graveyards, especially at night. He wondered why the old girl couldn't visit the place in the daytime like other people.

"He wasn't even worth it," Harry mumbled to himself.

Harry had not liked his late employer, and William Colby had not cared for Harry. Harry found out just how much the older man hated him when William Colby's will was read. The rich s.o.b. had not left Harry one cent. But the woman had assured him that she would keep him on as her chauffeur and that she would remember him nicely in her will.

Harry's problems with his employer had begun about three years earlier. He was not sure what made the man's attitude toward him change, but he had a good idea. It was probably that crazy girl. She was fifteen then. That Sonya was a wild one. She had really seduced Harry.

She had begun coming on to him with all kinds of seductive gestures, including patting him on his butt when no one else was around. What could a man do?

True, he was the adult in the situation and should have been the one to say "No," but Harry just could not find it in his power to do so. She assured him that she knew how to protect herself, so what could happen? The worst would have been for her parents to find out about them. For whatever reason, that had not happened. Or, if they had found out, they never confronted him about it. Maybe the old man was so busy doing his own thing he didn't have time to notice.

Well, William Colby was dead now, and there was nothing he could do about anything anymore.

Harry looked up in the rear view mirror at the figure in black that huddled in a corner of the back seat. She still wept, sobs shaking her frail body.

"Bless her crazy soul," he whispered.

The woman was still mourning, after all this time, for a man who had walked out on her for another woman. *I don't ever want to love anyone that much*, Harry thought.

He felt completely safe with the woman. She became a bit more eccentric by the day, but she was still the same kind and considerate person she had always been. He suddenly felt a pang of guilt. The woman in the back seat was to be pitied.

Harry had been in the employ of the Colby family, as Mrs. Colby's chauffeur, for ten years. Ten years of making the easiest and the most money he had ever made in his life. He washed the car more than he drove it—a little trick he had learned to make himself look busy. Mrs. Colby's limousine was undoubtedly the shiniest in town and the one with the least miles on the speedometer.

The lady was a real homebody. She shopped maybe once a week, made one trip to the beauty parlor a week, and two to the health spa. She even kept up this weekly schedule after the old man ran off with his younger woman, right up until he croaked. Then everything stopped except an occasional trip to the beauty shop. She had just let herself go.

Harry remembered how attractive Claire Colby had been before her husband's affair with the other woman began. She was so chic in her expensive clothes (clothes that now hung loosely on her body because she was so thin). Her face, that was always flawless and well-groomed, was now lined with wrinkles that seemed to have appeared overnight. Harry thought the woman had the most luscious pair of lips he had ever seen. The warm smile that she once flashed so freely from those lips was now gone. Those blue-green eyes that he thought were so enchanting were now vacant and sunken in her head; that beautiful, shiny, red hair was now almost completely white. She seemed to have aged twenty years in the last two.

Harry had gotten a glimpse of the other woman in his employer's life once when William Colby's personal car was in the garage for repairs. The man actually had the audacity to ask Harry to drive him to his woman's house in his wife's car.

"Don't mention my destination tonight to anyone, Harry," the older man said as he got out of the car in front of a row of newly built, luxury condominiums. He then handed Harry a twenty-dollar bill.

"I don't remember a thing," Harry said.

That was when he had become curious and decided to wait and see what the old boy was up to. So he hung around until they came out of the building to take a taxi to whatever awaited them that evening. What the street lamp enabled Harry to see, from a safe distance, was astonishing. No matter what the lady was, she was one of the most beautiful women Harry had ever seen. To Harry, his employer and his woman had looked very much like two people deeply in love.

Except... Well, Harry had often wondered about his tall, handsome, distinguished employer. For him to be a White man, his complexion was extremely dark, like a permanent suntan. Dark blue—almost black—piercing eyes, the thick lips, the jet-black hair—until it had begun to gray.

Maybe Harry should have blackmailed the cheap bastard. If he had known the man was going to die so soon, he would have. He certainly had the goods on him. William Colby had left his beautiful wife for another woman even more beautiful. But William Colby was White—supposedly anyway—and the other woman was Black. Love. It sometimes made people do crazy things.

Harry always dreamed of the woman with whom he would someday fall in love and spend the rest of his life. But not in poverty. He vowed that he would always have some money in his pockets. That was why he had left his home in South Carolina at the age of eighteen in search of a better life. He had heard that people made real money for their labor up north.

"So why don't you go north, Harry?" he asked himself one day.

That night, he hopped a train that was headed north.

"Real money," Harry said out loud and immediately wondered if the woman in the back seat had heard. He glanced at her in the rear view mirror. No, she had not heard. She was too consumed with her own thoughts.

"Poor soul," he whispered. As beautiful as she had been, she could have found someone else. *She should have divorced Colby and gotten on with her life*, he thought.

Love could mess a person up sometimes. And that was why Harry always let the women in his life do the emotional part of the love thing. He just did the physical, and that seemed to always satisfy them.

Harry ended up in the mid-west, and for the first four years, things were pretty rough. He went through ten jobs during that time, and none of them paid the money he thought they should. He had almost convinced himself he should continue further north when he happened to spot the Colby's ad for a chauffeur in the paper. He had heard that some rich people paid their chauffeurs exceptionally well.

Harry applied for the job and got it. He had lived well ever since and thoroughly enjoyed the fringe benefits.

Although Harry still had not found the woman of his dreams, he had made plans for his future. He decided he was going to play on the girl's shallow intellect and his power over her to make himself a rich man.

Sonya Colby was captivated by him. Women always were. They loved his body. That was why he worked out daily. He had to keep his body in shape for the women—all six feet, one inch, one hundred and ninety-eight pounds of it. Some said he was handsome in a rugged sort of way. He guessed he was. They even liked his gray eyes. As one told him once, "They make you look mysteriously romantic."

Harry's broad face lit up in a big smile. Whatever that was, he was glad his eyes did it for him.

Yes, the girl wanted him. She could not keep her hands off him. He very seldom had a chance to stay in his own room in the servants' quarters anymore. At her insistence, he had practically moved into her spacious upstairs bedroom. When the time was right, he planned to issue the little slut an ultimatum. Even if their marriage only lasted a couple of years, that would give him enough time to set himself up for life.

The drive to the Colby mansion on Forest Lane East was a treacherous one. Harry could barely see through the windshield. The wipers could not compete with the raging rain. He finally got the black limousine safely into the driveway. He pressed the button, and the automatic garage door went up. Harry drove the car into the four-car structure.

"We're home, ma'am," he said.

"Yes," the woman whispered.

How many times had he driven her to and from that graveyard at all hours of the night? Harry could not count the times.

He had sat in his room many a night waiting to see if she was going to call him to take her out there. During the first few months, the trips had been so frequent, and she stayed so long, kneeling there at the man's grave, talking to him as if he could actually hear her. Harry had been tolerant at first. But he had no idea the nocturnal visits to that ungodly place would continue for so long.

Now here they were at the end of that journey once more. Tonight had been about the worst yet. If he had not gone to the grave to get her, she might still be there, kneeling, talking to a dead man while a violent storm raged all about her.

Harry swore under his breath as he helped the woman out of the car. His clothes clung to his body, and he was cold—no, he was freezing. *I guess all this comes with the job*, he thought. At least the woman had a heart.

They entered the house through a side door that opened onto the mudroom. They went through to the kitchen.

"Good night, ma'am," Harry said.

"Good night, Harry." Claire's voice was almost inaudible.

Harry glanced at the woman beside him with her head down, her hands clinched tightly in front of her, her mind... God only knew where. He felt sorry for her, but there was nothing else he could do. His day was at an end.

Harry turned and went hurriedly in the direction of his room.

Claire's clothes were ruined. Water dripped from them onto the kitchen floor. The front of her dress was muddy where she had knelt at her husband's grave in the rain. She looked about the room. The house was quiet. Matilda, the cook, had probably gone to her room the minute the storm began. She loved to prop up in bed with a book and a cup of tea when it stormed.

Such a peaceful, uninhibited life, Claire thought. She had always been fascinated by how little it took to make some people happy. With all she possessed, she could not remember the last time she had been truly happy. It seemed so long ago—an eternity.

"I have to get out of these wet things," she whispered to herself. Then she thought, *what does it matter?* Nothing mattered anymore. Her William was dead. Gone from her forever. The permanence of his leaving her this time was too much to bear.

Claire went to the refrigerator, pulled out the vegetable drawer, and took out an apple. She loved apples and ate at least one every day. Nice and cold. The chilled, sweet flavor was so satisfying. Her mother always told her that apples would make her healthy, and as a little girl, she had become addicted to them. She closed the refrigerator door, pulled out a drawer beside the refrigerator, took a butcher knife out of it, and then left the room.

The thin figure of the girl stood at the top of the stairs. Moving. Always moving. Shifting her weight from one foot to the other. Her long, jet-black, hair—just like her father's—was disheveled. Her blue eyes blazed. Her beautiful face was contorted in an ugly sneer. She was only eighteen, but the hatred she harbored within her had already begun to fester.

"You look like something the cat dragged in." Sonya spat the words at her mother. She wanted them to hurt. "You've been back there again, haven't you, Mother? Whining over his grave. When will you ever learn?"

The girl moved back into the darkness of the upstairs hallway and disappeared into her room. Claire continued up the winding stairs then moved slowly down the hallway, in the opposite direction, to her room.

The child just doesn't understand, she thought.

Sonya Ellis had been born to Claire and William rather late in their lives, after they had given up hope of ever having a child. Claire was in her late-forties at the time. The delivery had been a frightening one. They were told not to try to have more children.

The child had been a blessing. They had given her William's name, as Claire's mother and father had given Claire her father's middle name. They had both looked like their fathers. They had both been "daddy's little girls." Except Claire's father had stayed with her and her mother until he died—as he had promised in his marriage vows to her mother.

Claire and William had adored their daughter. Consequently, they had spoiled her—special schools… birthday parties at the Ritz… They catered to her every whim. Sonya turned out to be a rotten child just as Claire's mother predicted.

Claire entered her bedroom and closed the door behind her. She walked over to the bed, and her body sank heavily onto it.

Sonya lay in her bed looking up at the ceiling. The door opened, and Harry slid through it. He had changed into

17

a pair of pajamas—red—Sonya's favorite color. She had bought them for him. A matching robe hung loosely about his shoulders. Harry closed the door and locked it.

Sonya's angry eyes met his. "Why did you take her?"

"She's my employer. I do what she wants," Harry said.

Sonya smiled wickedly, her anger gone or masked. Harry never knew which. She stretched out her long legs and patted the bed beside her. "I'm your employer, too, and I want you right here. Now."

Harry let the robe fall from his shoulders to the floor and began to take off his red, silk pajamas.

Claire had changed into a white nightgown and now sat on the side of the king-sized, four-poster, bed she had once shared with William. The butcher knife was in her right hand, the apple, in her left. Her eyes stared straight ahead at, perhaps, the antique white wall before her. She had sat like this for sometime now. Her thoughts were full of Sonya, her little girl. She had loved and cherished the child so much. Too much. Claire knew this now, but it was too late. All the hatred within the child... She and Harry... What would become of her little girl?

Claire's thoughts drifted from the girl. Whatever her daughter was, Claire knew she could not change her now. Her William was dead, and that was all that mattered. She tried to remember the last time he had held her and told her that he loved her. So long ago. So long. Before the other woman. No, she would not think about that woman. He would have soon gotten tired of her and come back home. Claire knew he would have. Her heart told her so. If only he had lived. If he had not left. There were so many ifs.

There just was not enough time. Time had run out for both of them, Claire and William. They had been the ideal couple once. Esteemed in the community. They were constantly invited to political and social events. They were of the elite crowd, the country club set... They had even attended a function at the White House. William had received the "Humanitarian of the Year Award" that year. He had fit right in with all the other dignitaries, even the president. She had been so proud of her husband. But, then, he had thrown it all away for another woman.

"You promised, William," she said, tears streaming down her face. "Until death do us part."

Her left hand moved slowly toward the night stand where she laid the plump, red apple.

She raised the knife in her right hand, tilted back her head, and sliced her throat.

CHAPTER 2

The blood-curdling scream stirred the entire house. It was the piercing shrill of a woman's voice.

Callie, the maid, was the first to enter the room from whence the terrible sound came. As she went through the door to Claire Gene Colby's bedroom, she spotted Harry coming out of the girl's room down the hall. He wore only a robe that was thrown carelessly about him—in haste, of course. Callie wondered if he always slept in the raw, and with the girl. She also wondered when Mrs. Colby was going to put a stop to their depraved behavior right there in the house for everyone to see.

The girl was a slut, plain and simple.

Callie's thoughts stopped short as she glimpsed the scene before her. Her screams instantly blended with those of Matilda's.

The other woman was backed up against the far wall. Her hands, made into fists, were wedged into the sides of her face. Her face was aghast, and her eyes were glued to a spot on the floor in front of her. Her screams now choked in her throat while Callie's went on fresh and anew.

Harry rushed into the room and instantly tasted bitter gall. "Dear God." The words forced themselves out of his mouth.

The two women now whimpered, a lamentable duo.

A soft-boiled egg; two strips of turkey bacon (Claire had stopped eating red meat at her doctor's suggestion); a slice of buttered, whole grain, raisin-cinnamon bread; a glass that once held orange juice; and an empty coffee cup lay on the floor beside an overturned tray.

The three sets of eyes stared at the lifeless body of their employer.

Claire Gene Colby lay about four feet from what was to have been her breakfast. She was beside the bed on the white carpet, the portion surrounding her head now a crimson color. It looked as if she had carefully placed a red blanket on the floor and then laid her head upon it. Her throat was cut almost from ear to ear as if the hand that held the knife had a perfect pattern to follow. Congealed blood clogged the hole in her neck. Her lifeless eyes stared grotesquely at some point beyond them.

Sonya was the last of the Colby household to enter the room. She looked at her mother's body and fainted.

"...and I will dwell in the house of the Lord forever. Let us pray." The minister closed his book, bowed his head, and began to pray. "Our most gracious, kind and loving God..."

It was a dreary day—cold, cloudy, and threatening rain. Only a few people attended the funeral of Claire Gene Colby: Sonya; Maurice Forrister, the Colby family's lawyer; Harry; Matilda; Callie; a few women from the William E. Colby Agency (who had come out of respect for their late employer); Claire's friend, Sylvia Madden; and the Reverend Marshall Jenkins. This small group stood over the open grave.

Claire had very few friends, and those few were so infuriated by her pathetic clinging-vine attitude when her husband so openly began his affair with his mistress, they had abandoned her one by one. All except Sylvia Madden. Sylvia had tried to remain Claire's friend, although she confessed to Claire that Claire's groveling demeanor toward William was so demeaning, it was an affront to womanhood. Sylvia came to visit faithfully for a while—until the day she suggested that Claire see a psychiatrist. Claire had graciously, but firmly, asked Sylvia to leave her house.

Claire never saw a psychiatrist, however. After all, she thought she was perfectly sane. She simply loved her husband. Should not every wife?

Claire had not missed her former friend's absence in her life. It was too full of thoughts of her precious William and hope that she refused to let die.

Matilda had called Sylvia Madden and told her about Claire's death, and Sylvia had come to the funeral to give the daughter her condolences.

"We now commit Claire Gene Colby's body back to the earth from whence it came. Amen." The minister looked up at the few people grouped on the other side of the open grave. His eyes came to rest on the stony face of the woman's daughter.

"She's at peace now," he said softly.

Sonya's face did not change. She did not speak. Her gaze seemed to penetrate his being. She looked on beyond him, through him, as if he were not there. He wondered if she had heard any of the words he had spoken over her mother. When had he ever seen such hate? Surely never, and certainly not in the eyes of someone so young. What was troubling this child? It was not her mother's death, he was fairly certain of that, for her eyes had remained dry throughout the service back at the church. Even now, while the coffin was being lowered into the ground—a practice that was very seldom done nowadays, but the girl had insisted— she exhibited no signs of true grief.

The maid and the cook had taken their employer's death quite hard. Perhaps they were thinking of being without employment now, but he did not think so. Their grief seemed genuine. But the daughter... The young woman had simply sat there with that strange look in her eyes. He knew that look, but not like it was being emitted from the face of this child. Pure hate. But directed at whom? God only knew. He wanted to help her, but he was not at all sure that he knew how. He had encountered some strange cases in his time, and this was certainly not the strangest, but it was about the saddest.

What could he do to help this young woman?

"The Lord knows best," the minister tried again to reach Sonya.

The girl's eyes still did not focus on him.

Why had she called him to officiate at her mother's funeral? He had no idea. Maybe First Methodist was the only church her family had ever attended. He remembered the family coming to services a few times, but he had not seen them in years. Mr. Colby sent offerings sometimes, and that was a blessing. He had heard about the father and the woman. All the gossip. He had always helped out wherever he could, whenever he was needed. This child was surely in need of help now but more than he was capable of giving he was afraid. He decided it would not be a good idea to try to comfort this young woman after all. He would let well enough alone.

The women from The William E. Colby Agency spoke briefly to Sonya. Sonya let her eyes rest upon them for a few moments, her only acknowledgement of their presence. The women turned and left the gravesite.

Sylvia Madden took Sonya's hand in both of hers. "I'm so sorry, Sonya," she said. She spoke briefly with each of the servants, and then moved on.

The minister moved over in front of Sonya. "God bless you, child," he said and quickly walked on to join the departing women. He had done all he could, what he had been paid—and quite handsomely—to do. The girl had been most generous.

Maurice Forrister touched Sonya's arm lightly. "I'll talk with you tomorrow," he said, then turned and walked hurriedly to his car.

Harry took Sonya's arm. She pulled away from him, her eyes flashing wildly.

"Leave me," she snapped. "All of you! I want to be alone with my parents."

Harry, Matilda, and Callie did as their new employer told them and headed for the family car.

Sonya stood looking down into her mother's grave. She stooped, picked up a handful of dirt, and threw it on top of the casket. Then she spoke, and her words were not kind.

"Well, here you are, Mother, beside him, where you have been aching to be for so long. You were weak, Mother. You were such a pitifully weak woman. You left yourself wide open for so much abuse, and he heaped it on. First her, then the company. Why did you let her have the company, Mother? Why didn't you fight? But I'm going to make her pay for all of it. Everything she has done to our family. She will pay. Just you wait and see.

"As for the family plot, well, the two of you can have it, because I won't be using my spot. I refuse to be buried on the other side of him, Mother. I'm not the feeble person you were. I didn't continue to love him. You let him shit on us! My body still reeks with the stench of it, because it won't wash off.

"You never learned how to hate, did you, Mother? Now here the two of you are in the graves you bought so long ago—husband and wife, resting together in death as in life? That's a mockery, Mother. But I guess you're happy now. Are you happy, Mother? Does this really make you happy? You know who should be here beside him, don't you? Yes, you know. We all know. That Black bitch that lay beside him while he lived!"

Sonya stepped over to the other grave that held her father's remains and spat on it. Then she turned and left the gravesite.

The funeral car pulled into the driveway of the Colby estate and stopped. The driver got out, went around to the passenger side, opened the door, and helped Sonya out of the car. He then opened the back door, and the three members of the Colby household staff followed from the back seat.

The undertaker took Sonya's arm, attempting to accompany her into the house but was stopped by the girl's icy stare.

"That will be all," she snapped.

The man looked in wonderment at the beautiful, not grief-stricken, but enraged young woman before him. "Good day, ma'am," he said. He turned and walked back around to the driver's side of the car, got in, backed the car out of the driveway, and drove off down the street.

The stately, brick mansion that loomed before Sonya and her household staff looked a bit ominous with the clouds hanging overhead. Sonya led the way up the walkway toward the front door.

The door had barely closed behind them when Sonya turned to the people who had been a part of the Colby family—some of them even before she was born—and snapped, "You're all fired! Pack your things and get out! Now!" She turned from the three panicked faces that leered at her and hurried up the stairs.

Callie was the first to find words. "You can't fire us!" The distraught woman's voice followed Sonya down the upstairs hallway. "You can't do this! We've been faithful."

Sonya's bedroom door slammed, shutting out Callie's last words.

"The slut," Callie hissed. "The filthy, sex-crazed strumpet."

"Hush, Callie," Matilda said. "Don't talk what you don't know."

"I know," Callie said. "Oh, yes, I know." She turned to Harry who had not moved from his spot at the bottom of the stairs. He still gazed up them. "Tell her I'm right, Harry. Tell her that gal ain't nothing but a piece of White trash. A rich whore! Only she doesn't sell. She gives it away. Probably buying some too. Ain't that right, Harry? Ain't it?"

Harry turned and left the women there at the foot of the stairs.

"Go on, Harry!" Callie yelled after him. "I know all about you! I know more than you think I do! You thought you had it made, didn't you? Well, you must not have been as good as you thought, because your dirty White tail just got canned the same as mine! How do you like that, Mr. Highfalutin? Tell me! How do you like that?"

"There's no sense in saying all those things," Matilda told Callie—who looked quite mad about now.

"I'll get even," Callie said.

Matilda's face clouded. She had seen the same crazed hate destroy the child upstairs. Yes, it was time she moved on. She had known it was time the morning she found Claire Colby on the floor of her bedroom with her throat cut by her own hands.

She had been with the Colby family for thirty-seven years. She was old now—seventy-five. It was time to retire and spend some time with her grandchildren. Really get to know them. She had seen that good White woman into her grave. There was no more she could do here even if the girl wanted her to stay.

Matilda remembered the sunny day she had appeared on the Colby's doorstep with her daughter in tow. They must have looked a sight: a tiny African-American woman and a pretty, half-Indian, nine year old girl, both of them cold and hungry after three days of hitchhiking from the reservation in South Dakota where they had lived until the girl's father died.

They sneaked off in the middle of the night, because the tribe did not want to let them go. But Matilda Barnes and her daughter, Bright Eyes (the father's name for his daughter), alias Andrea Barnes (Matilda's name for her), did not belong to anybody. They would be free to go and come as they pleased. Matilda vowed that she would see to that, and she had. Apparently she had chosen the right place to escape the tribe, because she and Andrea were never found.

Claire Colby—bless her soul—took one look at the bedraggled duo, hustled them into the kitchen, fed them, gave Matilda the job of assistant to the cook and Andrea the position of assistant to the assistant to the cook. Matilda knew that neither position was really needed until the cook, Marsha Washington, died two years later. But they had jumped in with both feet: Matilda doing what Marsha

26

instructed her to do, and Andrea taking out the trash, sweeping the kitchen and back hallway, polishing the silver, and setting the table with fine china, crystal, silver, and lace tablecloths.

They both got a good education in that kitchen. Andrea was also encouraged by Mr. Colby to do well in school. He even paid for her college education. Andrea went on to become a big-time engineer. Had a job making "big-time" money, too—as Matilda always said, teasing her daughter about her six-figure salary. Andrea also got married and had two beautiful children.

Yes, it was time Matilda got to know those children better. It was time she seriously considered her daughter's invitation to come and live with them. She had been thinking a lot about retiring lately anyway. It was funny sometimes how things just worked themselves out.

Claire Colby had told her that she was remembering all of her staff in her will. For that, Matilda was grateful. She had also managed to save most of her salary. She was determined not to be a burden to her daughter and son-in-law. She would invest her money wisely, make money, and pay her own way. She had never sponged off anybody and was not about to start.

I guess Mrs. Colby knew that girl wouldn't do right by us, Matilda thought.

Matilda's thoughts turned back to the enraged woman beside her. "Come on, Callie," she said. "There's nothing left for us to do now but pack our things and go." She tugged at Callie's arm, and Callie let herself be pulled toward the back of the house, her eyes still glued to a spot at the top of the stairs.

"I'll get even," Callie said again. "Just wait. You just wait and see."

Sonya sat at the desk, in a corner of her bedroom, writing in her checkbook. She would give each of them two weeks severance pay and the reference letters her mother wrote before she cut her throat. That was all that was required of her. That was all she would do. She finished writing the checks then picked up the phone that sat beside her on the desk and dialed. "I would like to make reservations to fly to Paris as soon as possible," she said after a moment. A moment later, she said, "One way."

After a brief conversation, Sonya hung up the receiver, hurried into her huge walk-in closet, and began pulling down pieces of luggage from a top shelf. She dragged a trunk to the middle of the floor and opened it. Then she began pulling clothes off racks. There was no order to her packing. She simply threw the clothes in the direction of the trunk and the nine pieces of Cartier luggage.

Sonya had made the decision to leave the country the morning her mother's body had been found. There was nothing to stay in Baltonville for now that her mother had killed herself, coward that she was, leaving her eighteen-year-old daughter to fight the family battle—a monumental task that Sonya knew she was not prepared to handle. Not yet. But she would be. She would finish her education in Paris then come back and do what she had to do—deal with the woman who had destroyed her family.

"What do you think you're doing?" Harry inquired from the doorway.

Sonya looked up into the man's angry face. "Get out!" she snapped.

Harry stepped into the room and closed the door behind him. "You know you don't mean that." He moved toward her, a smirk playing on his lips. "If you want to get rid of the women, fine. We can stay here, just the two of us, and have a great time."

He grabbed her, pulled her into his arms, and tried to kiss her. Sonya struggled against him, bringing her fingernails down one side of his face.

Harry grabbed his face. "You filthy, little—"

"Get out of my house this minute!" Sonya ordered, interrupting him. "You mean nothing to me! So you introduced me to sex. So what? If you hadn't, some other man would have. It was fun, Harry, but it's over. You were only a convenience. You're not even my servant anymore. You've been fired. Now get out!"

He slapped her. She slapped him back. They stood, each trying to stare down the other.

"If you ever touch me again, I'll call the police," she finally said.

"I'm going," he said. He backed away from her, pulled a handkerchief from his pocket, and held it to the injured side of his face. "You'll wish for me one day, baby," he tried one last time.

Sonya chuckled. "I doubt it, Harry." She extended an open palm. "Your keys."

Harry reached into a pocket, extracted a ring of keys, and threw them at her. They landed at her feet. Sonya picked up an envelope from the desk and threw it at the departing man.

"Your severance pay. I don't want you to have any excuse to come back here ever again."

Harry picked up the envelope from the floor and left the room.

The door slammed behind him.

Sonya took a moment to compose herself. She picked up the keys from the floor and put them in one of the desk drawers. She then collected the other two envelopes from the desk, left the room, and went downstairs.

Harry finished his packing. *Just like that, it's over,* he thought. All his dreams. How could he have been so stupid as to think he could control the girl with his maleness? How dumb can a man be sometimes? He should have known better. He knew the girl was a kook, capable of most anything. All that time… It had meant nothing to her. Just an experience. A game. A child playing grown-up games. And she had won. The little slut had used him.

"Well, this is over, Harry," he said to himself. "It's time to move on." Where, was his problem.

***

Moving on was not in Callie Foster's immediate plans. *If that gal thinks that envelope she just gave me and that little money her mama left me in her will is going to satisfy Callie Foster, she's as crazy as her mama was,* Callie thought. "That White gal doesn't believe fat meat's greasy. I guess I'm just going to have to show her," she said out loud.

Thoughts of how she was going to accomplish that task were already forming in Callie's mind.

CHAPTER 3

Callie Foster had grown up on a farm in Dexter, Missouri. She was the seventh of twelve children born to Sylvester and Lucille Foster. The first four, two boys and two girls, had died shortly after birth. Then Sylvester and Lucille had finally gotten it right—or wrong. Sometimes Callie wondered which. They were poor, uneducated, Black people—and when you called a Foster child black, that was exactly what you meant— black.

"Lord, they sure are black," one neighbor would say.

"But they're pretty, though," another would counter.

Callie knew the first statement was true and believed the latter with all her heart and soul.

Callie often wondered what her parents could have been thinking when they decided to marry and have children. Her ancestors had come all the way from Africa (she guessed), gone through slavery, and had not been diluted one bit in the process. But Callie did not mind. For, as the people said, the Foster children were the prettiest, little, Black folks they had ever seen: soft, smooth skin; keen features; even, pearly white teeth; and long, naturally curly, jet-black hair.

Callie still wondered about that hair. Something other than African must have sneaked into their family somewhere along the line, although it did not show up on the outside—just went straight to the top of the head.

Her color sure did not wane her popularity with the boys though. Not a bit.

"You're one fine little thing," came out of the mouths of many suitors.

Yes, Callie Foster was fine, and she knew it. In addition to the boys, her mirror and the jealous stares of some of the other girls told her so. One girl even asked her what she did to keep her size six figure so perfect.

"I don't have to do a thing. It just comes naturally," was her answer to that. What she thought but did not say was, *I don't eat like a pig like you do.*

The Fosters were proud but simple people. They contented themselves with a little five-room house, a cotton patch, some hogs, a few cows, chickens, and a garden. The girls helped their mother around the house, in the garden, and with the chickens; the boys helped their father with the hogs and the cattle. Everybody helped with the cotton—planting, chopping, and picking.

Sylvester Foster prided himself on being a good provider, and Callie supposed he was. She never went hungry, and she always had nice clothes to wear (most of which her mother made out of flour and feed sacks). But she never saw the inside of a restaurant, and her first store-bought dress was for her eighth grade graduation.

Callie had never seen her parents as proud as they were on her graduation day. She knew just how proud they were when they took her downtown to buy her graduation dress.

"This is an auspicious occasion," her mother said at breakfast that morning. Lucille loved finding big words in the dictionary and then trying them out on the family.

"It's a whale of a day if that's what you mean," Sylvester said.

They all laughed. Her parents were fun sometimes. But Callie did not want to end up stuck like they were. Country life did not set well at all with Callie Foster. She had to find a way to break out of what she called southern captivity.

Later that day, the family went into town where Sylvester bought Callie the most gorgeous dress she had ever seen. It was white chiffon with a taffeta underskirt and lots of ruffles that swayed when she walked.

She felt like a queen.

Callie took a bath in an old, number two tub on the big day. She dusted her body with her mother's dusting powder and splashed herself with Jasmine toilet water. Then the moment arrived—putting on her new dress. Callie did so although it was several hours ahead of time. She spent those hours admiring herself in the cracked mirror over the dresser in the room she shared with her four younger sisters.

Because this was Callie's special day, she was allowed the privilege of sitting next to her mother in the front of the family's old pickup truck. The other children sat in back on a blanket that Lucille had spread on the floor for this celebrated occasion.

"We're so proud of you, Callie," Sylvester said as he drove the truck away from the house.

"Amen," Lucille chimed in.

Callie had never felt so grand.

The little, country school that doubled as a church on Sundays was crowded that evening. Everyone was there: the parents, other family members and friends of the graduates, and both the Baptist and the Methodist ministers and their wives—all dressed in their Sunday-go-to-meeting clothes. And, of course, Callie could not forget the White folks, now could she? There were the superintendent of schools and the president of the board of education. Those two distinguished gentlemen showed their faces once a year. They congratulated Callie and shook her hand. *Probably wash all the skin off their hands when they get home after all this shaking*, Callie thought.

Education was the angel of mercy that won Callie her freedom from the dull country life she hated so much. After her graduation from the eighth grade, Callie's parents sent her to East St. Louis, Illinois to live with relatives. There, she was to get a big-city, high school education.

"They've got better schools there," Sylvester said.
"Be good, Callie," Lucille said.
Callie vowed that she would.

City life was a big disappointment to Callie. The East St. Louis relatives had six small children and lived in a two-bedroom apartment in what was called project homes. The rooms were so small, the entire family could barely fit into the living room at the same time (the room where they huddled at night to watch the ten-inch black and white television set, the only luxury in the house).

Callie shared a bedroom with the three girls. Her aunt and uncle had the other bedroom, and the three boys slept in the living room on a worn sofa that let out into a bed.

There were many nights Callie had to go to bed hungry, because there simply wasn't enough food. She found that she welcomed her mother's boxes from home every few months. They contained clothes for her, a couple of smoked hams, canned food from the garden (wrapped, and wrapped, and wrapped, so the jars would not break), and cookies. They had a feast whenever a package came. Callie was happy to see her city relatives enjoying the country food. *I just wish they didn't enjoy it so much*, she thought. *Then it would last longer.*

Callie's uncle did the best he could with the small salary he made working on his steel mill job. Callie's father also sent what he could toward her support. He was working on odd jobs, picking up what little money he could, he said. Sylvester did not mind, because it was going to be used for the best of purposes, his daughter's education.

"How do you manage?" Callie asked her Aunt Clara one day.

"The best we can," was her aunt's reply.

Thus, Callie's first big city revelation: more money was needed to live in the city than in the country. Armed with this newfound knowledge, Callie knew she had to search further for the new life of which she dreamed. She could not afford to live in the city, and she sure wasn't about to go back to the country.

Callie stayed with her relatives for a little over two years. In her junior year in high school, she met a man who offered her a better life.

Walter Underwood was an eighteen year-old high school dropout. But to Callie, he appeared to be better off than most of her teachers at the school. He had a good job, money in the bank, and a car.

Callie and Walter dated for a couple of months before her aunt and uncle found out about them. When they discovered Walter was not in school, they had a fit. Her uncle said Walter would never amount to a hill of beans and demanded that Callie stop seeing him or he would tell her parents.

Well, Callie did not stop seeing Walter, and when he asked her to marry him a few months later, she said yes. One of his friends printed her a false birth certificate stating that she was eighteen, and they eloped. Walter told her how much he loved her, and Callie vowed that she would make him a good wife.

The happy couple moved into a three room, shotgun house that Walter bought for them in a little town called Brooklyn, some six or seven miles east of East St. Louis. They had a living room, a bedroom, a kitchen, and a bathroom. They went shopping for furniture, and Callie enjoyed fixing up the place. Her mother had taught her to sew, so in order to save money, she made draperies for the windows and slip covers for a sofa and a pair of chairs they found at a secondhand store. (Lucille would have been proud of her daughter.) Callie bought pictures to hang on the walls, bric-a-brac and other ornaments to set about. Walter praised her for the good job she was doing.

"I sure did marry a smart woman," he told her.

Callie smiled and graciously accepted his praise. She thought that if she liked school better, she could probably be an interior decorator someday.

Callie was also a good cook, and did Walter love to eat. Callie would prepare big dinners. One of his favorite meals was: fried chicken, collard greens, black-eyed peas, fried okra, candied yams, macaroni and cheese, corn bread, and apple pie. Callie cooked. Walter ate, and Callie could see that once hard, brawny body that she had fallen almost in love with turning into a big blob of disgusting, flabby fat.

Callie did not like fat men.

The not so newlyweds lived happily for a while— until Callie discovered they were headed in the same direction as her parents and her East St. Louis relatives. She made this discovery about a year and a half after they were married. She awoke one morning nauseated. No one had to tell Callie Foster-Underwood what that meant. She knew all about babies. That, she had learned in elementary school from her girlfriends.

Callie found a doctor to help her out of her predicament. She used the money she had saved from household expenses (another little trick she had learned: Always have some money stashed away for emergencies). Her husband was a generous and trusting man.

Callie decided that school and the institution of marriage held about the same fascination for her. She had no use for either. One day, after Walter left for work, Callie did the quickest packing she was sure any woman had ever done. She set her bags out on the front porch, went back into the house, called a cab, went to the bank, took all of the money out of her and Walter's joint savings account, and disappeared.

She had not heard from her husband since. She had not made any attempt to contact her family either, because her father had renounced her when she quit school and got married. He had written her the angriest letter.

"I wash my hands of you!" he said. "You've made your bed, now sleep in it the best you can."

And that was that.

When Callie left Walter, she had no idea where she was going. Baltonville, Missouri turned out to be the lucky place. Because Walter's world was so small—Brooklyn and a few other surrounding cities east of the Mississippi River—if she played her cards right, she didn't think she would ever come face-to-face with the man again. Baltonville was on the other side of the river. It was a big place, and she was going to get lost in it.

Luck was not on Callie's side in the big city. Jobs were not as easy to come by as she had thought, and the ones she did find were not at all what she wanted, but she had to live. She did day work for the so-called middle class White folk between other jobs as a dishwasher, a short order cook, and a school janitor before assuming the position of maid with the Colby family two years later. The job was still not what she had in mind for herself but better than all the rest. The pay was good, and she would be staying right there in the house—a good place to hide, just in case.

The Colby house was like no other Callie had ever seen even in her wildest dreams. After seeing the Colby mansion, Callie decided those other folks she had worked for did not have much more than she did.

"Do you have any references?" The rich, White lady asked when Callie applied for the job at the Colby house.

"I certainly do," Callie said and produced the perfect reference letter (that she had written herself) from her supposed last employer in another state. All the drilling in penmanship, spelling, and grammar had not been a total waste. She had to thank Mrs. Garrett, her English teacher.

She was hired.

What Callie did not know about working for the really rich, she would bluff her way through. It did not take much to fool people, and she had found that she was good at it.

On her day off, Callie visited and became friendly with a few of the other maids in the community. In a short while, she knew her job thoroughly.

The Colbys were a decent sort of people, except for the girl. Callie had watched Mr. and Mrs. Colby spoil that brat rotten. Then after Sonya reached her teens, Callie felt sorry for her, because she knew the girl was headed in the wrong direction. Some of the stunts she pulled.... And then when she and Harry started getting together... She probably had a few of those wayward boys who kept coming around in between, too.

Callie knew about the time it began with Harry. There wasn't much that went on in that house that she did not know about. *That man ought to be horsewhipped*, Callie thought. She was shocked that the mother and father chose to ignore the obvious. The rich certainly had peculiar ways, Callie finally decided.

Callie felt sorry for Mrs. Colby when her husband took up with his other woman. A Black woman, no less. No, African-American. (Callie forgot that they had changed it again.) *Someday, maybe they will decide on something and stick with it*, she thought. But what in the world was that African-American woman trying to prove with that White man? No matter how good he might have been to her, he was still White. Callie was on the daughter's side, where that issue was concerned. She detested the little slut, but the girl was right about her father and the woman. Callie shared the feeling, for basically the same reason. White folks weren't the only ones partial to their own.

Now the little wench had fired her, after all those years, and given her two weeks severance pay and a note to call that lawyer to get the ten thousand dollars Mrs. Colby had been decent enough to leave her in her will. But Callie wasn't satisfied with the Colby handout. Not by far. Matilda and Harry might be, but Callie was going to show that little

38

hussy that she could not kick other people around and get away with it.

Callie knew the Colby family was headed for some kind of disaster long before they did, so she had begun preparing herself. When the girl asked her to hand over her keys, she almost laughed in the little slut's face.

Nobody got over on Callie Foster. Nobody. The Colby family would be her ticket to success.

Having a duplicate key made to the servants' entrance was one of the smartest moves she had ever made.

CHAPTER 4

Callie decided she would sneak back into the house that night after Sonya had gone to bed—to sleep since she had gotten rid of her live-in stud. Callie laughed. The ignorant man really thought he had it made with the little slut until the shit hit the fan.

Callie had plans to become permanently self-sufficient, and the Colby house was going to help her accomplish that goal. *I'm going to enjoy this*, she thought.

She went around the house toward the servants' entrance. Just as she rounded the corner, a car drove up into the driveway. Callie came back to the corner of the house and peeked around the side. The illuminated lights on top of the vehicle told her that it was a taxi. The car stood in the driveway with its motor running. Callie saw the driver get out and go toward the front of the house. In a few moments, he reappeared with several pieces of luggage. He went back again and again. The last time, he brought out a large trunk.

After a lengthy struggle, he managed to get all of the luggage into the trunk and the back seat. Sonya appeared, and the driver helped her into the front seat. He got in on the driver's side, backed the overloaded vehicle out of the driveway, and drove off down the street.

Callie ran around to the front of the house and watched the taillights of the car until they disappeared.

"Well, where is she going?" Callie asked herself. "With all that luggage, she must be planning to stay awhile." She laughed. "Well, well, well. That makes it all the better."

Callie raised her eyes to the heavens. She wanted to yell, but, instead, she said quietly and reverently, "Thank you, Lord."

Callie went back around to the servants' entrance, unlocked the door, and went into the house. She went to her old room and sat quietly for about an hour—just in case the girl came back for some forgotten something. Callie couldn't imagine what that could be though, since it looked like she was trying to take the whole house with her.

Callie came out of the room and went down the hallway to the dining room. She picked up a candle from the table then went on into the kitchen where she pulled out a cabinet drawer and fumbled in it until she found a book of matches. She lit the candle then went on through the living room and up the stairs to Sonya's bedroom.

She opened the door and stepped inside. Her foot hit an object on the floor just inside the door. She tilted the candle down to see better, and stood for a moment surveying the mess on the floor around her: discarded clothes, shoes, scarves, handbags, jewelry... *Probably junk she didn't want to take with her*, Callie thought. She certainly wasn't going to clean it up. Callie, the maid, had been fired.

Callie stepped around the mess on the floor as she made her way into Sonya's practically empty closet. She smiled as she said to herself, "If I had planned this whole thing myself, it could not be better organized. The little slut has really left town."

Wherever she's gone, let her stay, Callie thought. *She won't be missed around here none.* "This changes my plans though. Yes, indeed," she said to herself. She threw back her head and laughed. "Things are looking up for Callie Foster!" she shouted. "Yes, they are!"

After Callie's inspection of Sonya's room, she went down the hallway to the bedroom of the late Claire Colby. She stopped outside the door as if to compose herself for the ordeal ahead. After a moment, she bravely opened the door and went inside. She flicked a switch beside the door, and light filled the room. No one could see the lights from the street in this room like they could in the girl's room. She had to really use her good common sense like her daddy taught her in order for her scheme to work.

Callie set down the candle on a table just inside the door, and then folded her arms across her chest as if to ward off a sudden chill. She moved stealthily about the room, her eyes searching every corner, falling momentarily on every item enclosed there. They found and lingered on the spot on the floor where Claire Gene Colby had lain that horrible morning.

At least the child had the good sense to have the room re-carpeted. All that blood could never have been cleaned up. A new white rug. *White folk sure do love their color. It's a wonder money ain't white*, Callie thought.

When Callie's inspection of the room ended, she went over and stood before a picture that hung on the north wall. She removed the awesome looking piece of artwork to reveal a wall safe. She set the picture down then rubbed her hands together in anticipation, her eyes glued to the safe. She knew the combination. She had for years. Claire Colby had opened that safe many times in her presence. The woman would just walk over and start turning the dial as if Callie wasn't even in the room.

It's amazing how some people regard others as nothing, Callie thought. The rich, especially, think they're the only ones. And if you're a servant, to them, you sure ain't nothing.

"Nothing. Just a commodity. No feelings and no brains. Right? Wrong," Callie said to herself. Not Callie Foster. Callie had brains, and right now, she was using them.

Callie began to turn the combination lock on the safe, and, in a few moments, it clicked. She opened the door and reached inside. She pulled out a jewelry box, set it on the dressing table, and opened it. Inside, sparkling in all their brilliance, were the expensive gems Callie had helped the other woman put about her neck, on her wrists, and on her fingers so many times.

Callie began trying on the jewelry, one piece after the other. She marveled at herself in the mirror. "Not bad, Callie," she said out loud. "Not bad at all. Splendor becomes you."

Callie awoke to the sunlight shining on her face through the huge bedroom window. She had pulled the top draperies open the night before just before retiring. She had lain in the king-sized bed, in her new ermine trimmed gown, and watched the moonlight shining through the trees until she drifted off to sleep.

Callie thought being mistress of the Colby manor might be fun, and there was no better way to begin than by sleeping in the former mistress' bed. It was a nice bed. It was so comfortable and the prettiest thing Callie had ever seen—one of those four-poster things with a canopy over it. She used to make it up and visualize herself asleep in it or propped up reading a book with all the silky finery draped about her.

Dreams do come true, she thought. Why the woman had put a knife to her throat, Callie could not understand. No man was worth that, no matter what. That was rich folk for you.

Well, she was going to see what being rich would do for her. Certainly no crap like it did to the Colby family: the husband running off with another woman, the wife killing herself, and the daughter... God only knew what was going on in that child's head. She was surely messed up. Of that, Callie had no doubt.

"God, what a mess," Callie whispered.

She sat up in bed, her mind racing. Now that the circumstances had changed, there would have to be a few alterations to her plan. First, she would go to the run-down motel where she had deposited her meager belongings the day before.

"No, no, why would I even want that crap?" she asked herself out loud. "Forget that. I'll never wear another cheap dress or another pair of bargain basement shoes as long as I live." Why should she when the closet in her new bedroom was filled with expensive, fashionable, free clothes—and in her size? She chuckled to herself. The shoes might be a little small, but she would manage until she got her money together. "I've got to go see that lawyer first thing Monday morning," she said to herself. "I'll get that ten thousand stashed away while I put my new plan in motion."

Yes, Callie was going to have money and lots of it. Her day had finally come, and she was looking forward to it. She was finally going to see how the other half lived. "The cat is slowly crawling out of the bag. Yes, indeed," she said to herself.

Callie was sure the utilities would stay on at the house, so she would not have to worry about that. The water was needed so the gardener could maintain the grounds. *I'll just have to keep out of his way*, Callie thought. And the electricity was needed so the lights outside would continue to come on at dusk. "To keep intruders away," Callie said out loud and chuckled to herself. "So I'll be safe."

And there's enough food in this house to feed an army, she thought. The freezer in the kitchen and the one in the basement were stuffed to capacity with all kinds of meat and other frozen foods, and the cabinets were running over with canned goods.

She would cook as little as possible, use candles at night, and try to duplicate her actions every month so the bills wouldn't look suspicious. That lawyer would probably be paying them, but she didn't think he would pay much attention to how much they were, since it wouldn't be his money paying them. The telephone, she could do without. What she did have to worry about was that lawyer snooping around the house. If Sonya left keys with anyone, it would be him.

Well, she would just have to outfox the man. *That won't be hard to do,* she thought. Callie Foster could match wits with that fat, ugly, red fart any day. Most men of his caliber thought they were so smart anyway, they outsmarted themselves sometimes.

Callie chuckled to herself, got out of bed, put on the matching robe to her exquisite, designer gown, and went downstairs to make herself some breakfast. She would serve herself on the best Colby china, bring it back up to her new boudoir on a silver tray, and eat out on the balcony overlooking the gardens.

From now on, Callie Foster was going to receive the queenly treatment she deserved.

CHAPTER 5

Velma Hannah sat at the dressing table in her bedroom. She was thinking about William, about the company, the office that had been hers for over six months now—since William died. He had stipulated in his will that she was to take his office as well as his position. She had his name taken off the door and her name put up right away.

Velma liked her new position as general manager and half owner of The William E. Colby Advertising Agency and enjoyed the power that came with it. She was determined to run the company as if William Ellis Colby were still in the driver's seat. She and...the girl. As much as she wanted to do so, Velma could not forget the younger woman. They were heiresses-in-common. The agency was as much the girl's as it was hers, but an acting assistant general manager was still occupying the office at the other end of the hallway.

Sonya had not been inside the building since months before her father's death, since the day she found Velma in his arms in his private office.

"I could kill you!" the enraged girl had screamed. "Both of you!"

Velma would always remember the pure hate that filled the younger woman's eyes.

William had run after his daughter who had turned and fled the office.

Sonya had gone home and told her mother, and there had been a big scene. Sonya had screamed obscenities at her father and told him to get out, to go back to his Black bitch. His wife had pleaded with him to stay. Although they had not been living as husband and wife for a long time, she was still hoping they could work things out between them.

That night, William moved into a hotel. He later bought one of the units in the building where Velma lived—a complex of exclusive, high-rise, apartments turned condominiums—and moved in on the floor above her.

William asked his wife for a divorce. She refused.

Velma could see how agonized William was over what had happened. She suggested they not see each other anymore except in a professional capacity at the office, but he would not hear of it.

He talked with his wife periodically after he moved out of the house, but his daughter completely ignored him. William loved his daughter and kept trying to win back her love. He had expensive gifts shipped to the house for her—whatever he thought she might like and appreciate enough to at least call and talk with him. Sonya would open the gifts, discover they were from her father, destroy them, and mail them back to him at the office. A diamond bracelet came back with all the diamonds plucked out of their sockets and black dye poured over them. A note in the box read: "Give these to your Black whore. They would look good tacked to her ass."

When William died, Sonya did not bother to come to the reading of his will. Her mother and the family lawyer had to tell her about her inheritance, and she told them what they could do with her half of The William E. Colby Agency. She would not have gone to her father's funeral if her mother had not pleaded with her so pitifully.

William's funeral was held on a weekday. Velma did not go to the office that day. She did not go to the funeral either, but it took all of her willpower to stay away. She knew she belonged there, because she was the woman William had loved. She also knew that she owed his family the courtesy and respect of staying away. Consequently, she denied herself the opportunity to look upon the face of her beloved William one last time.

The day after William's funeral, Velma found a grotesque, black, papier-mâché wreath tacked to the door of her condominium. She knew that, somehow, Sonya had gotten into the secured building and put it there.

Now, the girl's mother was dead, also. Suicide, the papers said, and in the worst kind of way. Had William suspected that his wife would die within months of himself? Was that why he had made Velma promise to look after his daughter?

Velma had tried to tell him the futility of such a thing. She reminded him of how Sonya hated them, and her especially. But he insisted that the girl would understand someday and need someone. As far as he was concerned, Velma had to be that someone. "If something should happen to my wife," he had said.

Had he known that his wife was capable of taking her own life? Velma wondered. She thought now of the last words he had spoken to her as she stood over his hospital bed: "Take care of my little girl."

Velma had promised. A few minutes later, William Colby had a fatal heart attack.

Claire Colby had been called. She came right away. She was beside Velma before Velma knew that she was in the room. Claire turned to Velma, and Velma could see the hurt, the suffering, and the grief in the other woman's eyes. A brief feeling of overwhelming guilt besieged Velma. Then Claire Colby spoke, and her voice was soft but stern, determined, and perhaps a bit threatening.

"He's my husband. I will take him now." She turned from Velma, dismissing her with the gesture.

Velma had no choice but to move away from the man she had learned to love with all her heart. William Colby had been one of the few men who had understood and respected her. He was, indeed, one in a million.

Velma watched as Claire Colby took her husband's hand and began to stroke his face. She watched as the woman's head fell to William's chest and as she began to weep, calling his name softly—over and over. She watched as the woman slid to her knees beside the bed, her agonized cries filling the room. Velma watched until she could no longer bear to do so. With a feeling of not belonging, she finally turned and left the room.

Velma did not go back to her condominium that night. She could not—knowing William would not be coming home, and that she would not get her nightly phone call from him just before he retired. She checked into a hotel, but she did not sleep. Instead, she lay awake all night trying to decide her future.

Velma had not heard a word from the assistant general manager of The William E. Colby Agency. Of course, she had not expected to hear from Sonya in spite of what William had said. In spite of all of his hopes and dreams for his daughter.

"Had he really believed that she would need me?" Velma asked herself out loud. She doubted it, and if Sonya did ever need her, Velma was sure the younger woman would never admit it. Sonya would go to her grave hating the woman she thought had stolen her father's love. Of that, Velma was sure.

Velma had tried calling the Colby residence but was told the telephone had been disconnected. She had a feeling something was desperately wrong. She considered going out to the Colby house but had immediately thought better of the idea. Velma wanted to carry out her friend's dying wish but had no idea how she was going to accomplish that task.

Her memories of William were so strong. She had truly loved the man. *Ironic that his last words to me, the woman he professed to love, were of his daughter*, she thought.

Velma Hannah and William Ellis Colby had been employer and employee before their alleged affair began. Velma was one of many secretaries at the multimillion-dollar ad agency. She had seen the man who owned the thriving company for which she worked in passing and at the monthly company meetings many times. Shortly after she began working for the agency, she had been asked to stand, along with a few other new employees, at one of the meetings and had been introduced to William Colby from afar. She had not met him formally, however, until the day she was called into his office for an interview for the position of his personal assistant.

When the job opening was posted, Velma had put her name on the long list of applicants. She hoped she would be the one to get the job. The increase in salary was enormous, and she could certainly use the money, but she was a bit doubtful. There were so many qualified applicants.

On the morning of her interview with William Colby, Velma sat before the sprawling mahogany desk, surrounded by walls plastered with degrees, certificates, awards, pictures and plaques—all proclaiming the importance of the person who occupied the office. Velma was even more dubious about her chances of getting the job after learning more about what the job of personal assistant to William Ellis Colby entailed. The person who assumed that position would have to be top-notch. Velma did not doubt her ability to handle the job, but she knew some of the other applicants were just as capable as she.

Approximately fifteen minutes into the interview, William leaned back in his chair, tented his hands, and said, "Out of all the applicants who applied for the position of my personal assistant, Miss Hannah, you are the best qualified."

"I am?" Velma blurted, and immediately wanted to slap herself for losing the professionalism she had possessed so naturally for so many years. She had promised herself she was not going to be awed by this man simply because he was rich and powerful—and also her employer. "I mean, uh, thank you," she stammered.

"Congratulations, Miss Hannah," he said. He stood and came around the desk, proffering his hand.

Velma rose and took his outstretched hand. "Thank you," she said again.

"I'm sure we'll work well together, Miss Hannah."

"I'm certain we shall, sir."

Velma knew deep down inside that she was, indeed, capable of filling the position she had just secured.

Her Hubbard's Business College training was finally paying off. And being on the dean's list didn't hurt either. This made up for all the rigorous studying she had done while the other girls in the dorm partied and had fun.

"You're here to get an education," her father had told her when he deposited her at the school. His old Chevrolet station wagon had started to sputter and cough the day before, but he was determined to drive those one hundred and thirty miles, so his daughter could begin her college education. He had prayed over the car, and, miraculously, it had made it.

"Study hard, and it will pay off someday. Never lose sight of your goal," were his departing words of wisdom to his daughter.

Yes, Velma knew she would be a competent personal assistant to William Colby, but standing there with the man, at that moment, with her hand in his, she felt grossly inadequate—until he flashed his winning smile.

William Colby had a way of putting people at ease in his presence. He had an air about him that said, "Relax, I'm only a man."

Velma had been attracted to William from the beginning. Before long, she knew the feeling was mutual. God knows she had not meant for anything to happen between them. She was an African-American woman and had sworn, for as many years as she could remember, that all a White man could ever do for her was give her a decent job and pay her what she was worth.

But life was surprising at times. Velma had learned that fact early in life. Whenever she was faced with a problem and approached her father, a Methodist minister, for answers, he always said, "Just another challenge. Life with all its intricacies is sometimes hard to explain."

She never thought though that her true awakening to that fact would be so profound.

Velma had known many men since she began dating at the age of sixteen (for where she came from no self-respecting Colored girl ever started dating—let alone necking and petting—before the age of sixteen, and especially a preacher's daughter).

She dated African-American men, her kind of men, she always told herself. The only kind for her. Ever. She would make at least one of her relationships work. And she had tried. For more years than she dared remember, she tried. She was beautiful, talented, and had personality to spare (her father always told her). She attracted men by the droves. They came, stayed awhile, and then they left her. Some of them married other women. Two left her for White women, and she had blamed the women. Finally, Velma admitted to herself that she was just unlucky in love, as were many women—and men—for that matter, but she, especially.

Velma wasn't sure what her problem was with men, but she had a good idea. She realized that most men were not willing to embrace her ideals, and she was not willing to compromise.

She had almost given up on her search for the right man—until William. William Colby was one man who never questioned her about her beliefs, and that was one of the reasons she had loved him so much.

After she had worked as William's personal assistant for about six months, William had begun to confide in her. He talked about his life and how unhappy he was. How he and his wife had grown apart. How he had moved into a spare bedroom. How inadequate he felt as a father and as a husband. How he wanted out of his marriage—but he did not know how to extricate himself without hurting his family.

Velma knew she was falling for the man. She knew the feeling well. She told herself, "No," but everything within her said, "Yes." There was something about the man that was irresistible. He was so innocent, so vulnerable, and yet so powerful, so all-consuming.

Velma seemed drawn to him and found that she could not help herself. She thought about quitting her job, the best-paying job she ever had. She could not do that. She would just have to work it out somehow. After all, she was a grown woman. Surely she could do a better job of controlling her emotions. And she tried. God, how she tried.

William had been fighting, too—fighting his feelings, as Velma was hers. Velma could see this in the way he looked at her sometimes, looking quickly away whenever her eyes met his. She saw it in the way he threw himself into his work as if trying to substitute work for the inevitable. Was it destiny that they should be together? Velma was not sure. What she was sure of though was that she had been powerless to fight it.

They worked well together, and the job at the top demanded more and more of their time. Velma's social life was about nil anyway, so she felt she had nothing to lose. She enjoyed her work and was learning the business from the top. It was an exhilarating feeling.

Eventually, their working late and dining together went from strictly business to events to which they both began to look forward. Velma wasn't sure how it happened, but, one day, they found themselves in each other's arms.

She had dreamed of his lips on hers many times. But when it finally happened, the guilt was so strong for both of them. Guilt that left them cautious. Wondering. Guilt that put them in a predicament with which to deal was not easy. They wanted to be together, but they both knew that it was wrong, because he was still a married man. But they could not reverse what had finally happened. They did not want to reverse it. They had to find a way. But they had to do it the right way. William had to get a divorce so they could be married.

Then the girl had seen them kissing in his private office, and Velma wasn't sure that she was sorry. She wasn't sure that William had been sorry either. It was a relief for both of them that the surreptitious meetings, the stolen hours together, were finally over. William had put off asking his wife for a divorce, because he said she was so fragile and dependent upon him. He was waiting for the right moment.

Well, Sonya had solved that problem for them.

William tried to do the right thing, for his wife, for his daughter, and for her, the woman he loved. He wanted to spare his family, and he wanted to spare Velma—for she would surely be condemned as "the other woman" who had broken up his marriage. An amicable divorce would have made things look so much better for everyone concerned.

William said he could withstand the stares, the disgust displayed on the faces of his and Claire's so-called friends. But the one thing he could not, would not do was give up the love he had found with Velma.

But his wife had said "No" to a divorce.

The ringing of the telephone brought Velma out of her reverie. She punched the speaker button. "Yes?"

"Good morning, Miss Hannah," her secretary Delia Summers' voice came over the instrument. "I just thought I'd remind you that you have a meeting with Accounting at nine."

"Thanks, Ms. Summers. I'll be there in twenty minutes." *What am I doing?* Velma thought as she released the button. She had completely forgotten about the meeting with Accounting. And...she should have been at the office at least forty-five minutes ago. She was pushing herself much too hard, but she would have to carry on as usual until the other half of the company decided what she was going to do.

Velma had expected Sonya to do something—as wrong as that something might have been. But the silence, the nothingness, disturbed her. She knew the younger woman was capable of most anything. Why was she so quiet? What was on her mind? The mind of a normal eighteen-year-old could possibly be invaded, flushed out, and maybe straightened. But Sonya... Sonya was not a normal eighteen-year-old by any standards.

Velma suspected Sonya had something planned. But what? When would she reveal her hand? How would she? Whatever, Velma knew it would be designed to hurt her. She had expected Sonya to cause all kinds of trouble right away. She was not naïve enough to think the girl would just walk away and give an outsider her father's company, inheritance or not. Of that, Velma was sure.

Velma Hannah's inheritance was a bitter one, but she was not about to give it back.

CHAPTER 6

It was Saturday night, and there were candles everywhere: large ones, small ones, and medium sized ones. They were on tables, mantles, and inside the light sockets in the chandeliers. The house was ablaze with them. In the dining room and the den, the party was well under way. The music was loud and inviting—foot-stomping music, music that made one want to dance. And they danced—all fifty, or so, of them. They ate from the elaborate, delicious-looking buffet of every delicacy imaginable—except that Caviar crap. The White folk could keep that delicacy all to themselves. Black people wouldn't be caught dead putting raw fish eggs in their mouths.

They drank from the silver champagne fountain that flowed continuously and the many bottles of fine liquors the hostess provided.

Callie was the perfect hostess. She mingled among her guests: the African-American maids, cooks, butlers, and chauffeurs from an approximate ten-block radius of the Colby manor and a few from across town. The known snitchers among The African-American Domestic Engineers Society had not been invited.

Callie had taken great pains preparing for her party. She shopped, going from one delicatessen and gourmet shop to another, buying any foods she thought her friends would like. Then on to the liquor store where she bought a case each of champagne, Scotch, bourbon and gin. She brought the fountain, which she had set up for the Colbys to use so many times at their formal gatherings, up from the basement for the champagne.

It had been nonstop for three days: shopping, cleaning, getting ready for the big bash—an affair no one among Callie's select group of friends would ever forget. Callie made sure of that. She wanted everything to be perfect, and it was.

Callie's guests were all dressed in their best discount store and hand-me-down fashions—formal attire, of course—and costume jewelry. Cheap perfume, cologne, and sweat mixed as they moved to the beat of the music.

A genuine smile was pasted on Callie's face as she made small talk and coaxed her guests to have the time of their lives. Not one of them disappointed her.

"You look radiant," one of the men (the butler from next door) said as he passed Callie on his way back to the bar.

"Thank you, Carl," Callie beamed.

She knew she looked just that—radiant. Her dress was from Saks Fifth Avenue. It was an off the shoulder, black sheath with a split up the front. A diamond brooch adorned the front of her gown. On her ears were small diamond earrings; and on her fingers were diamonds, emeralds, and pearls. A pair of black satin pumps graced her feet. They pinched and pained but looked simply elegant. Her hair was piled high on top of her head in a most becoming style—the result of a visit to the beauty shop earlier that day. She had chosen Bal A Versailles for her fragrance for the evening (a provocative French perfume—she had read somewhere). Whatever the fragrance was going to provoke, Callie was ready for it.

The compliments had started coming her way when her first guest arrived, and Callie was eating it up.

She had decided that a party was just the thing to indoctrinate her into her new role as mistress of the Colby mansion. The true owners had not wanted the place, it seemed. One had killed herself, and the other had run off to God only knew where and left the stately manor unattended.

What a shame to just let the place stand idle. Such a magnificent structure should be lived in not left to rot.

Of course, Callie was thinking of herself more than the place. Why shouldn't she? She deserved all this and more. And she was having more fun than she thought was possible in a lifetime. She felt good. No, more than good. She was ecstatic. She felt important. She felt rich, and one day, she was determined she would be.

Maybe she was a Cinderella, and the Colby house was her fairy godmother. But she would not have any midnight mishaps like poor Cinderella. There would be no midnights for Callie Foster ever again, just the brightest of days.

Callie continued to make preparations for her new life through very careful scrutiny. She found a man who would buy all the jewelry she brought him for a good price, no questions asked.

She had already gotten rid of some of the gems and had plans to get rid of a lot more. Some were her favorites, and had been for years—when the other woman had worn them. Those she would keep.

She would never work another day of her life. She would invest her money and let it work for her. Just like those White folk were using her, she was going to use their valuables to do for her. Only her slaves would be green. The only resemblance to a human her slaves would have would be the face of some ugly joker sitting smack dab in the middle of every one of them, and they all just happened to be White. She would love flashing their ugly mugs around.

In due time, she would move out of the Colby house, leave the city, and buy a mansion of her own. Maybe she would go to Spain, go back to school—God forbid—learn to speak Spanish, get a hair weave—all the way down to the middle of her back—and become a wealthy Spanish senorita.

The music stopped abruptly, and Callie left her thoughts to look up and see Joe Wilkins over at the turntable. He changed the record, and the sounds of a slow, love tune (what Joe called belly rubbing music) filled the room. Callie knew what that meant. Joe wanted to get close to her. And that was all right, too, because she liked him a lot.

They had been dating for over four years and had some great times together. He was the chauffeur for the Brentleys two doors down, so they saw each other quite often.

The Brentleys trusted Joe completely with their car, and that worked out just fine for him and Callie.

Sometimes, after Joe dropped the Brentleys off at a function that he knew would last half the night, he and Callie would jump sharp and parade around town in the limousine. The windows were tinted, so no one could see them. Sometimes they would drive over into the next town and have dinner or go to a movie. Sometimes they would have one of Joe's friends chauffeur them. Those were the times they really laid it on thick, especially Callie. She thoroughly enjoyed the stares from strangers who thought she and Joe were somebody. And, indeed, they were, if only for a little while.

Yes, Joe was a lot of fun, and Callie really did enjoy him. There was just one thing: now that Callie was starting a new life for herself, she was going to have to forget about Joe Wilkins, because there was just no way he would fit into her plans.

Sorry, Joe, baby. I guess that's just the way the ball bounces, she thought.

Then Joe was at her elbow. "Let's rub a little, baby," he whispered, his mouth close to her ear.

"Rubbing's my style," Callie said, smiling up at him.

He stood a good foot taller than she, and Callie liked that. Tall, Black, and handsome was the way she described him. He wasn't as black as she was but almost. Callie often wondered what their children would have looked like if they had met when they were younger and gotten married.

She slipped into his arms, and they joined the other couples, who had already gotten a head start belly rubbing, on the floor. Callie liked the feel of Joe's solid, muscular body against hers. No flabbiness about him in his middle age. He worked out and kept fit. Callie liked that about him.

She liked a lot about Joe Wilkins, and she was going to miss him.

Callie and her guests did a lot of belly rubbing and whooping it up that night. They were in one of their whooping stages when Callie's best friend, Susie Moss, the maid at the Van Buren place a few doors down the street, came running up to Callie.

"The doorbell's ringing," Susie shrieked.

Callie went into an instant state of panic. "Are you sure?"

"Sure, I'm sure," Susie said. "I heard it."

"Oh, God!" Callie looked about in total confusion.

Take it easy, Baby," Joe said, putting an encouraging hand on Callie's shoulder.

"You've got to do something," Susie said.

"I know. I know."

"Well, what are you going to do?"

"I don't know."

"Well, do something," Susie urged.

Callie sprang into action. She moved swiftly about, shushing her guests. When they were all quiet, she turned off the music. She pulled the jewelry off her ears and fingers and handed the gleaming stones to Susie. Susie enclosed them in her hands then put her hands behind her back.

"Quietly disappear, everybody," Callie said.

They did.

Who would come here? Callie thought. The girl was gone. The girl. Somebody didn't know she was gone. Probably one of her fast-tailed friends that had come around every now and then. Although the girl didn't have too many friends. She was too busy playing house with Mr. Macho.

Whoever was at the door was apparently getting impatient from the way the bell was ringing now. Callie hurried through the living room. She had not thought about what she would say to this person, but she knew she had to answer the door.

The person on the other side of it had surely heard the noise and knew someone was home. She just hoped it wasn't that lawyer. That fat snoop had already been to the house for his monthly check-up of the place. And he wouldn't be ringing the doorbell anyway. He would just use his key and walk right in like he owned the place.

Callie looked through the peephole in the front door. She saw a woman standing there—an African-American woman. Callie prodded her memory but could not recall ever seeing this person before. Perhaps she was a friend of one of her guests. Then why didn't she go to the back door? Everyone knew. But, no. No one would have invited someone else without first checking with her. They all knew better than to do something like that. This woman would not fit into their crowd anyway. She looked, well, too sophisticated. No, this woman was not here for Callie's party.

Callie opened the door. "Yes?"

The woman stood before Callie—tall, slender and picturesque. Her clothes were the best—tantamount to Callie's wardrobe now—and she wore them in a queenly fashion. She was the most beautiful woman Callie had ever seen, Black or White. Callie hoped this stranger was not perceptive enough to sense that she was literally petrified.

"Good evening," the woman said.

"Good evening," Callie said.

"Is Miss Sonya Colby in?"

"No." Callie swallowed hard. She wished her heart, that was beating quite frantically about now, would quiet itself. Whoever this woman was, she did not know that Sonya had left town. "She's out," Callie continued. "I'm the maid, and I just got in from a party." She tried to explain away the dress and fancy hairdo.

"Oh? I'm Velma Hannah," the woman offered.

Callie caught herself before she reacted to this bit of news. She knew the name well. Velma Hannah's name had come up in the Colby house quite frequently during the last year or so. And how.

Callie thought that if this woman only knew the things Sonya Colby had said about her, she would try to put as much distance between herself and that girl as possible. Certainly wouldn't be coming looking for her.

Callie had observed Mrs. Colby who never said too much. She just sat around looking as if she had just been told she had two weeks to live. Then her hopes would soar whenever Mr. Colby called to say he was coming by the house for some reason. She would dress up for him, trying to look her best for the few minutes he was around—fighting a losing battle. And now Callie knew why. And the girl... She would always go to her room and lock herself inside after screaming a barrage of profanities at her father. (That girl could curse like nothing Callie had ever heard. As far as Callie was concerned, she could write her own book.)

And the servants were expected to walk around throughout all this pretending they had not heard a thing.

Callie heard all right—everything.

Then Mr. Colby had stopped coming. The lawyer began coming by instead, and all the packages to the girl started. What an outrageous waste of good money. Callie thought of a lot of things she could have done with all the money he spent sending that expensive stuff to that gal.

"I heard music and other noises and thought perhaps she was having a gathering of some sort," Velma Hannah continued, interrupting Callie's thoughts. "I didn't mean to interrupt, but I've been trying to reach her for sometime now. I thought maybe she could spare me a few minutes."

"Well, she's not here. I was playing some party records. Didn't get enough while I was out, I guess, and I wasn't ready to retire just yet." Callie laughed nervously as she told this lie.

"Party records?" Velma's voice was skeptical.

"Yes, records. I like to listen to them sometimes," Callie said as convincingly as she could.

"I see. Well, it's urgent that I talk with Miss Colby as soon as possible. Please tell her I'll call again tomorrow evening." Velma proffered her business card. "Here's my card," she continued.

Callie took the card and folded it into her hand without looking at it. She had to think fast. She did not want this woman coming back to the house tomorrow or any other night, or day, for that matter.

"I'm afraid she'll be gone for sometime, Miss," Callie heard herself say. "She's out of town, and I don't really know when she'll be back."

"Out of town?" Velma asked, surprised.

"Yes, ma'am."

"But that's impossible."

"No, ma'am. It's not."

"When did she leave?"

"A couple of days ago?"

"Where did she go?"

"I don't know, ma'am. She didn't say." Callie wished this woman would just go on and stop with all the questions.

"What did she say? Surely she told you something."

Persistent, Callie thought.

Velma was becoming impatient with the woman who stood before her. She was hiding something. She could tell.

"No, Miss Hannah. Nothing. Miss Sonya is rather peculiar at times."

"I see," Velma said. "Thank you."

"I'll sure tell her you're looking for her when she returns."

"Thank you. Goodnight." Velma turned and walked down the steps.

"Goodnight," Callie said. She closed the door and leaned against it for a moment. Her breathing was hard. She tried to compose herself. So that was the notorious Velma Hannah, the woman who had created all the commotion in the Colby house. She looked at the woman's business card.

There it was as bold as day: Velma Hannah, General Manager, William E. Colby Agency.

"She's in the driver's seat, all right," Callie whispered to herself.

Well, she could see how Mr. Colby had fallen madly in love with the woman. There was no wonder he wanted to divorce his wife and marry her. *Why, with her looks, that woman could have any man she wanted, married or not,* Callie thought.

Callie knew all too well what the woman wanted with Mr. Colby, but did Miss Hannah ever really think about what she was doing? If she wanted to be a White man's mistress, she should have lived back there when that bleached out devil had it all legal and proper to have his White wife and his slave women, too. Men. It was a wonder God didn't strike them all dead.

You don't hear too much about White men and African-American women, Callie thought. Just a few African-American women seemed to have taken leave of their senses. It was mostly the African-America men who usually went crazy over those White women. Some of them would pee all over themselves trying to get to that smelly piece of dirty, White tail that looked so bad sometimes their own men didn't even want it. *Our men will just have to learn some sense, and that's all there is to it,* she thought.

Well, that African-American woman did not pick William Ellis Colby up out of no gutter. No sir. That man was about as rich as they come except for maybe kings and queens, and that Trump fellow and the Kennedys. But he was still White, and it was wrong what Velma Hannah did to that poor woman.

Mrs. Colby didn't have a chance in the world. Not with a looker like that after her husband. White, African-American, or whatever, the woman had what it took to turn any man's head. At least she didn't have to worry about how she was going to make it from day to day. *So I guess I can't really compare her to the African-American men,* Callie thought.

Callie hoped the story she had told Velma Hannah had been convincing enough. If not, she did not think she had a thing to fear. At least Mr. Colby had not left his mistress his house. Darn near everything else though. Talk about wrapped, that woman had that poor—no, rich, filthy rich—man mummified.

Callie chuckled to herself. She went back through the dining room to the den, changed the record, and turned up the volume on the stereo. The sounds of an upbeat, foot-stomping tune filled the room.

"Let's party!" Callie shouted to her guests as she began to move to the beat of the music.

They did.

Velma drove away from the Colby house in her metallic gold Jaguar (the last present William had given her before he died). She respected his wishes, but trying to keep her promise to take care of his daughter was apparently going to be more of a problem than she wanted to even try to handle.

There is something strange going on inside that house, she thought. Sonya out of town. The maid standing there looking as if she had just stepped out of Vogue. That dress must have cost somebody a small fortune. Velma was sure she had heard a party going on: loud voices, music, and laughter. And she had glimpsed candles burning as far as she could see inside the house. Maybe the woman was performing some kind of ritual. Or, maybe the maid is just living it up while Sonya is away. "While the cat's away, the mouse will play," she said out loud and could not stop the chuckle that followed.

Velma wondered where Sonya had gone, and why she had gone and left her inheritance behind. For how long was she going to be gone? Why had she not told the maid where she was going? Why hadn't she at least called the agency and told somebody something?

Velma was not sure how she was supposed to proceed. She was merely half owner of the business. How much authority could she legally assert? When would Sonya come in and accuse her of overstepping her bounds? She was, in fact, the general manager, and Sonya was technically her assistant. There was really nothing she could do but continue to run the business the way she had been doing until the girl came to her senses and came on board.

Velma pulled into the underground parking garage of her condominium complex, parked the car, and took the elevator up to the tenth floor. She secured herself inside her home then picked up the purring animal at her feet and began stroking it.

Geronimo sat contentedly in his mistress' arms looking up into her eyes, savoring every stroke. Then they began to talk to each other: she, in her language and he, in his.

Velma had found Geronimo, beaten and half starved, three years earlier. He was wandering outside the apartment complex in which she had lived before she bought the condominium. She had taken him in and nursed him back to health. They became fast friends.

Geronimo seemed to enjoy his new home until William began coming over. Then he had become withdrawn, sulking like a jealous child, or lover. He would leave the room whenever William appeared and go to the bedroom that he shared with his mistress. He would be curled up in his place at the foot of the bed when she retired at night—not asleep, but waiting for her. After she was all tucked in, she could feel the bed move as he put his head down and relaxed. A few minutes later, she would hear his light, even snoring.

Her protector. She loved him, too.

Now that William was gone, Geronimo was back to his old self. He was her only companion again, and that seemed to make him happy.

Velma took the cat into the kitchen where she went about getting him some food and fresh water. Geronimo followed close by her side. After she fixed his food, she went on into the master bedroom. Geronimo ate then came into the bedroom where he waited outside the bathroom door while his mistress showered. She came out naked. Geronimo watched as she put on a long, flowing, sea green, nightgown (the same color as his eyes). He rubbed against her legs, purring contentedly.

Velma reached down and patted Geronimo's head, then mistress and cat went to bed—she, stretched out at the head of the queen-sized, plush bed; he, at his place, on the other side, at the foot.

I'll think about this mess some more tomorrow. I'm tired, Velma thought. She turned over on her side and went to sleep.

Callie's party continued until just before daybreak. Her guests could not be seen leaving the house, so when dawn threatened, Callie gave the word. The ones who had to work the next day, she had sent home earlier. The others, uninhibited by the thought of having to get up early, had partied on. But now, it was time to go.

"Okay, gang, get your butts out! Go back to those happy homes you live in where the White folk loooooooooves you so much," Callie yelled.

This brought uproarious laughter from the not so sober party crowd. They began to file out—tired but happy—through the back door, and went their separate ways. Some slipped around the garage, disappearing into the alley. Some went around the side of the house and onto the sidewalk. Some had driven—either their cars or the cars of their employers—and had parked their vehicles at least a half block away or in the alley. Some gave others lifts. Most of them walked.

Joe and Susie stayed to help Callie clean up the mess. Around nine o'clock, Callie let them out the back door, and then she went back into the house, up to her spacious bedroom, and fell across the bed. She would take the dress off later. Right now, she was just too tired.

CHAPTER 7

"She's in France."

"France?" Velma looked at the man who sat before her in complete surprise. "But why would she just leave the country without a single word to me?"

"That's Sonya for you, Miss Hannah. She doesn't think she has to explain herself to anyone."

"That's ridiculous. She and I have a business to run."

"Apparently that isn't one of her concerns right now." Maurice Forrister leaned back in the comfortable chair behind the desk in his plush office and laced his fingers. "She's going to school over there," he continued.

Velma was shocked. "Going to school? But she was to attend school here. Her father had it all arranged. She was to work part time at the agency, learning the business, while she attended the university."

"Apparently that has all changed, because she's going to school in Paris."

"But that's absurd."

"Is it?" Maurice smirked at Velma, enjoying the woman's chagrin. She was finally losing some of the poise she exuded when she walked into his office a few minutes earlier. "I have been counsel for the Colby family for over twenty years. I watched Sonya grow up. I can tell you firsthand that she has a mind of her own. She always has, and since her father severed the bond between them, it has been overly profound."

"He did not sever their relationship. He loved his daughter. She was all he ever talked about. He—"

"Not exactly, Miss Hannah," Maurice interrupted her. "There was one other person who took precedence over William Colby's daughter...and his wife."

"Meaning me, of course," Velma said. She was becoming more irritated with this pompous, aloof, insulting man by the moment. She had decided the night before to come see him. She thought if anyone knew what was going on with Sonya, that person would be Maurice Forrister. She had heard a lot about the man. The more she heard, the less she liked him.

"Yes, you, Miss Hannah." Maurice Forrister was enjoying himself. He thought of the man who had once been closer than a brother to him—until this woman. He would have to admit that he had not condemned William for leaving his wife for another woman, but because of his choice of woman. Maurice remembered his and William's last argument when William had dismissed him as his attorney and promptly obtained someone else to represent him and The William E. Colby Agency. This woman had not only caused him to lose a good friend, she had also caused his income to plummet—drastically.

Luckily, Mrs. Colby and the girl had asked him to continue to represent them. But just being the Colby family attorney only brought a fraction of what he had been making, and the reason was sitting before him right now.

"You were all William Colby really cared about, Miss Hannah," he continued.

"That's not true, Mr. Forrister."

"William's wife and daughter seemed to think so. Those were the people with whom I conferred after William deserted them. And the cause of that desertion was unequivocally you."

"It was not William's fault. He tried to keep in touch. He gave them everything they needed, and more."

"No. No, he didn't, Miss Hannah. Claire Colby needed her husband, and Sonya needed her father. You took that away from them—forever."

The man was trying to goad her, and she was determined not to let him. "I didn't take William from them, Mr. Forrister. William stopped loving his wife and directed that part of his life toward me. There was no initiative on my part. I did not ask William Colby to fall in love with me."

"It just happened. Right, Miss Hannah?" He chuckled. "Without any encouragement from you?"

"That's right."

"That's the way it always is, it seems," he said, a smirk playing on his lips. "Or that's what we lawyers are told anyway when we're asked to handle a divorce case that is the result of such a situation."

"I'm sure you hear a little of everything in your profession, Mr. Forrister."

"I do, indeed, Miss Hannah. People bring me their problems, and I do my best to solve them."

"I'm well aware of your track record."

"Impressed?"

"Not necessarily."

"Well, your opinion of me really doesn't matter." He smirked at her. "I'm sure as William Colby's," and he said the next word as despicably as he could, "*lady,* you have a most distorted view of me, especially after your married lover saw fit to discharge me as his lawyer."

"Be careful you don't need a lawyer yourself for defamation of character and slander, Mr. Forrister. After meeting you in person, whatever my friend, William, told me about you was definitely an understatement. I see now that William Colby was too much of a gentleman to speak words, and especially to a lady, that would adequately describe a man of your character."

Maurice looked at her, nonplussed.

"Let's get back to why I'm here. Shall we? The William E. Colby Agency," Velma continued.

"Yes, well, all I can suggest is that you carry on until Miss Colby decides to return to the states."

"And until she decides to assume her position at the company…?" It was more a question than a statement. "I'm sure you must know that she's assistant general manager in name only. She has to learn the business."

"I guess that's something the two of you will have to work out yourselves."

"I need to know what she plans to do about the business now. While she was here, she never set foot in the place. When she comes back, it might be the same thing all over again. You're her lawyer. You must apprise her of her responsibility to the agency."

"I'll do my best, but I assure you, that task won't be easy. I don't think she likes you as a partner, Miss Hannah."

"That's beside the point. We are partners whether she likes it or not."

Maurice Forrister told himself he did not like the woman who sat on the other side of his desk. He knew she did not deserve all that William Colby had lavished on her.

This was the first time he had laid eyes on Velma Hannah. He had heard so much about the woman. He had heard that she was beautiful, but this… He had never seen any woman quite so enchanting, and feisty, and… If she were not of another race, he might even consider playing around with her himself. Nevertheless, he could not condone his late friend's fascination with her to the point of actually thinking of marrying her. And then giving her half of his company. No self-respecting White man would have thrown away so much on a Colored woman. Maybe it was a good thing he died before he made a complete spectacle of himself.

He had certainly tried to talk his friend out of doing the stupid thing he had done, but William seemed to have taken total leave of his senses. It was as if he were bewitched, as if the woman had voodooed him. The Blacks were known to resort to such barbaric tactics. This woman looking at him with those gorgeous, bewitching, brown eyes, just might be a devil in angel's clothing. But a beautiful devil, indeed. He wondered how William had felt when

71

he... He was letting his imagination run amuck. Yes, the woman was lovely, and, yes, captivating, but he was not the weakling his late friend had been. If she was on the prowl for another benefactor, Maurice Forrister was not available.

Claire Colby had been a fool, also. He had tried to get her to contest the will, to fight for what was rightfully hers, but she wouldn't listen to him either. She might have won. He might have been able to swing it, to sway the judge's decision, bend the rules, break that unfair will. The company would now be Sonya's completely. And this woman would not be sitting in William's office acting as if she owned the world. That it was hers to do with as she pleased.

Why she even had the nerve to look down her nose at him. The disdain in her voice. Now that she had been taken out of her natural environment and thrown into a world where she did not belong, she would never be good for anything anymore: society, another man—definitely not a man of her own race. They wouldn't have a chance now that she had tasted of a White man and all the rewards that came with the package—extremely high stakes with William Colby. She couldn't be satisfied with the position he had given her. She had to have more, much more. So she had schemed, plotted, spread her legs, and stolen half of the man's company—and messed up a few lives along the way. A classic case of *give an inch, take a mile.* You just can't help some people. The ungrateful bitch.

He wondered if she had done something to induce William's fatal heart attack.

"The company will not suffer for lack of her presence there. It's just the principle of the matter," Velma continued.

Velma Hannah was not only beautiful, scheming, and cunning but smart as well. Maurice had no doubt that this woman could run The William E. Colby Agency without any help from anybody.

"Principle, Miss Hannah? You have the gall to speak of principles?" he said.

"I do, indeed, Mr. Forrister. The company is the issue here. My position there has been established. It's Sonya's that still remains in obscurity."

"I'm afraid I don't know what to tell you."

"Perhaps you can tell me how long she plans to be gone."

"A few years. Four at the most," he said.

"I see," Velma said. Her expression was disbelieving. "I just don't understand how she could simply walk away and leave her business—"

"In the hands of a stranger...?" he interrupted.

"I'm not a stranger to the company. I know more about that business than Sonya will ever know. And you seem to be forgetting that I am part owner."

"No, Miss Hannah, I could never forget the day my friend handed over half of a multimillion dollar company to the other woman in his life."

"Good. There's something else I would like for you to remember. This other woman will never give up her share of that company. No amount of money can buy me out, and nothing will ever run me out—just in case you and Sonya are thinking along those lines."

"I can understand your feelings, Miss Hannah. You must have put out a lot to get your name on those papers."

"Making unfounded assumptions about other people, Mr. Forrister? You, especially, should know better." She looked at him for a moment, and then continued. "What William Colby and I had was good and decent. I will not permit you or anyone else to spoil my memories. Your opinion of me is immaterial, and if I heard you right a few minutes ago, William felt the same way."

"Yes, you're right. William did not value my opinion either. Now Sonya is a different story. We get along fabulously."

"I'm sure you do. Sonya is a rather peculiar young woman, but I still find it hard to believe she would just leave the country without a word to me or anyone else at the agency."

"As you said, Miss Hannah, she's a rather peculiar young woman."

"But the house? The servants?" Velma looked at him in wonderment.

" The house is closed, and the servants have all been dismissed."

"Dismissed? But—" Velma began.

"Sonya closed the house and let the servants go the day she left town. The day of her mother's funeral, to be exact."

"That's impossible. I—"

"Miss Hannah, I believe I have told you all I can about this matter at the moment." Maurice's voice was impatient. "Either Sonya or I will notify you when she returns. I shall be conservator of her estate until then, so I'll be in touch with the company from time to time."

"I see." Velma rose. "Thank you for your time, Mr. Forrister. Good day."

She went hurriedly from the office. Maurice did not return her expression of farewell. He would not give her that satisfaction.

Velma was furious with Sonya, with Maurice Forrister, and, at the moment, with William Colby for putting her in her present predicament.

"Jesus!" she said out loud as she drove away from the office building. She thought for a few more moments then chuckled. *They're the ones who can't handle this, and that's their problem. I'll be darned if I'm going to buckle*, she thought.

"No way," she said out loud. "You're in this fight to the finish, and right now, you're looking like the winner. Yes, you are."

Velma drove out of her way to pass the Colby house on her way home from work that evening. She slowed the car and peered through the shrubbery that secluded the estate from the road. She saw nothing unusual. The automatic lights had come on, but there was no movement about the

74

house and no lights burning on the inside that she could see. It did, indeed, look closed. But Velma knew better.

If Sonya had let the help go, why was the maid still there? And why had she been so secretive? What had she been doing when Velma came by during the weekend? All dressed up in one of the most expensive dresses she surely had ever worn. If the woman had not told her she was the maid, Velma would never have guessed. She looked more like the lady of the house. And Velma knew she had heard other people, and it sounded as if they were having the time of their lives.

A party was going on inside that house that night, and Velma knew it. But the woman said she had been listening to party records. Velma would try to believe that.

The woman had also told her that Sonya had only been gone a couple of days, when, according to the lawyer, she actually left the day of her mother's funeral which was over two weeks ago. So who was telling the truth? As far as the maid's activities were concerned, whatever she was doing, Velma wished her well. As for Sonya, she would deal with that when she had to do so. With Maurice Forrister, she would not concern herself.

Velma's car sped off down the street leaving a trail of smoke in front of the Colby estate.

That night, Maurice Forrister made frenzied love to his wife. She was happier than she had been in a long time. He was as frustrated as he had ever been in his life.

Later, he dreamed of Velma Hannah.

CHAPTER 8

Velma got up early the next morning. She wanted to be the first to arrive at the office—a practice she had also inherited (for lack of a better word) from William Colby. He always came in especially early on days that he had scheduled meetings first thing in the morning.

The first thing on Velma's agenda this morning was a meeting with Creative. She had to straighten out a few things in that department. That division of the agency had begun a demise soon after William's death. She would have to put a stop to the problem before it got completely out of hand.

The problem, she knew, and he was going to shape up or else. "Just who does he think he is?" she said out loud as she turned onto Broadwalk Avenue. "Some people."

Velma had finally reached the decision that everything was on her shoulders. If the other owner of the agency had left the country without a word to her, she must have had great faith in Velma's ability to run the agency. Therefore, Velma would do what she knew was best. That would be all anyone, even William, could ask of her.

Her newly inherited position was turning out to be a lot more than she thought it would be—a lot more than it should have been. It wasn't fair that she should have to take on the whole burden of the company when she would receive only half the profits.

But, then, what was fair in life? The girl surely thought it wasn't fair that Velma had inherited into the Colby family business. Well, Velma had not thought it fair that

William's wife had not given him a divorce. As his wife, she would have been the legal heir. And...looking back on American history with all of its intricacies, who knew? William's ancestors might have gained access to their wealth, and the agency, through ill-gotten means—on the backs of, and through the direct efforts of her ancestors.

Who knew anything anymore? As it was, she had to bear the brunt of all the criticism, the degradation of being branded the other woman. The malicious gossip, most of it untrue. No one tried to understand that she and William had loved each other, that they had tried to do the decent thing. No one tried to see a decent side, only the worst.

Well, she knew what she was doing, thanks to William, dedication, and a lot of hard work. Because of his confidence in her, William had put her in the driver's seat. She would drive. Even if it meant rolling some heads.

Velma immediately thought of the head of Creative. "His is going to be the first to roll," she said to herself.

The William E. Colby Agency had one of the largest client lists in the world of advertising. The company occupied the five top floors of the Candry Square Building at Fifty-Sixty-Five Broadwalk Avenue. It had expanded to the top floor a year earlier. William had been ecstatic. They celebrated the expansion time and time again: at dinner, at concerts, at the theatre, or alone—just the two of them. She was happy, because he was happy. He was happy to have a woman who shared his excitement, he said.

Velma was glad to be that woman. She refused to even speculate what the woman before her had contributed to his life.

"I miss him," she said to herself.

A sleepy guard met Velma at the front door of the Candry Square Building. She had long since ceased having to show him her pass.

"Good morning, Miss Hannah."

"Good morning, Jim."

"Going to be a nice day."

"I believe so." She went on down the lobby to the elevators and punched the up button.

Velma stepped off the elevator on the twenty-fifth floor, and the company's head maintenance engineer was waiting for her.

"Good morning, Miss Hannah," he said.

"Good morning, Robert." She chuckled. "It is only I."

"Yes, ma'am," he said and laughed.

Velma went on down the hallway to her corner office. She was pleased with Robert Schultz's concern for the company. Robert met anyone who came up to the executive floor before the workday began.

He had ushered a few undesirables out of the building a few times and delighted in telling the stories. Everyone, even she, listened attentively as he recounted them, time and time again, as if they were hearing them for the first time. No one ever knew how much he was making up and how much was really the truth.

There was the time he had opened up one morning and found a drunk asleep in the hallway on the executive floor. It was assumed the man had gotten past the guard somehow and wandered in the day before and had been locked in the building all night. It was dead winter and cold. The man had no idea where he was or how he had gotten there—just that he had a warm night's sleep for a change.

Then there was the time a senile, old man had gotten past the guard and made it up to Executive. He had insisted that he was the president of the company and demanded that Robert show him to his office.

"That was a tough one, because we couldn't just throw the president out," Robert said and laughed harder than anyone. He said he finally convinced the man that his office was downstairs on the first floor. Then Robert had taken the man to the guard station where the man barked orders to all the guards until they managed to get enough information out of him to call his family. And on and on the stories went to the delight of all.

Robert had been with the agency since the beginning. From the way William talked about his head maintenance man, they had both started their careers at the agency together—William junking up the place, and Robert cleaning up after him.

William had loved the older man, and Velma had grown fond of him, also. He was one of the few people inside the agency who had not been concerned about what was happening in the lives of William Colby and Velma Hannah. He remained the same throughout, never voicing his opinion one way or the other. When William died, he had remained the same loyal and courteous employee to Velma.

There was something to be said about a person like Robert Schultz. He attended to his business and let that of other people alone. If only Robert Schultz's attitude could be duplicated about two hundred million times.

Velma unlocked her office door, passed through her secretary's office, and went on into the larger one. She closed the door behind her, and the deep red walls engulfed her. She went soundlessly across the plush, red carpet; past the antique white, Italian furniture; and on behind the huge white antique desk. She opened the draperies that covered the enormous window that practically ran the entire front wall. Then she sat down at her desk.

She had to plan her strategy for the meeting with Creative. It was to begin promptly at nine o'clock. This was one day everyone, in that department anyway, would certainly be on time for work. Maybe she should call surprise meetings of all departments intermittently and see just how many of her employees were dragging their feet.

She had seen a tremendous lax in attitudes and productivity since William died. The agency had lost some of its biggest accounts, and others were threatening.

Problems with that girl, amid everything else, are just what I need right now, Velma thought. Maybe Sonya wanted the agency to go under. Maybe that was her ploy. She was certainly not doing a thing to help keep it afloat.

But, then, Sonya could do without the revenue the agency brought in; Velma could not. The William E. Colby Advertising Agency was all she had going for herself, and she was determined to hold on to it.

Whatever it takes, she thought.

The sound of the buzzer startled Velma. She had heard her secretary come in earlier then leave again a few minutes later. She would have checked the conference room to see that it was in order for the meeting: leather-backed pads, glittering made-to-order silver and black pens at each place, and the built-in serving counter laid out with fresh coffee and French pastries. Everyone would be stuffing their faces by the time she got there. Breakfast. No time for even a cup of coffee at their various places of abode—not when a meeting was called at nine o'clock in the morning (although that was the time everyone was scheduled to be in place to begin work each morning).

Velma knew the call meant that Creative was assembled. She pressed the intercom button. "Good morning, Ms. Summers."

"Good morning, Miss Hannah. Creative is waiting for you," Delia's voice came over the intercom.

"Thank you." Velma released the intercom button, smiled, and stood.

Velma walked into the conference room— undoubtedly the most impressive looking room at The William E. Colby Agency. The paneled walls were adorned with several mounted moose heads, the head of a wild boar (that William had loved—an instant conversation piece), paintings, a coat of arms that bore the Colby family crest, and a portrait of William that hung over the head of the table. Around the magnificent mahogany conference table (that glistened as if William Colby were still around to monitor its gleam—and Velma intended to keep it that way) in deep brown, soft, leather chairs, sat members of the Creative Department. There were Chief Creative Director Bradley

Morris, the supervisors of the various creative groups, and Bradley's secretary—all, as expected, laughing, talking and stuffing their faces.

Velma conducted the meeting as professionally as possible considering the circumstances under which she was placed. Bradley's eyes had fallen upon her when she entered the room. They perused her. They laughed at her. They belittled her, as if trying to bring her down to size. Whose size? His?

Velma talked about the department's apparent lack of enthusiasm for the work they were doing, about the department's productivity level falling below the agency's expectations and needs, and how the agency had lost several accounts because of Creative's inability to produce. She told them that things would have to change in order to salvage what they had all worked so hard to achieve.

Bradley opened his loud mouth only to challenge every issue, to disagree with whatever she proposed to rectify the situation in his department, and to crack jokes—all of them inappropriate.

Bradley had looked down on her when she worked in personnel—before her promotion. But now, she was in charge. She was boss, everybody's boss, and especially his. The agency belonged to her, half of it anyway. Until the girl came to claim her half, she was Miss "It." He took his orders from her now. The sooner Bradley Morris learned that, the better off he would be.

When Velma tired of the whole demeaning affair, she adjourned the meeting and asked Mr. Bradley Morris to meet her in her office immediately.

The others left the meeting, following close behind Velma, moving hurriedly to the elevators and down the one floor to their offices to begin work.

All except Mr. Morris. He strolled slowly down the corridor to Velma's office, arriving at least four minutes after she had.

Velma paced behind her desk. She was furious. Of all the people at the agency, an African American man would have to be the one who defied her. "He'll do his job, or I'll can his ass," she said out loud.

Bradley strolled into Velma's outer office as if he had all the time in the world.

Delia looked up when she heard the door open. "She's expecting you, Mr. Morris. Please go on in."

"Thank you, Ms. Summers." Bradley continued his stroll through the secretary's office. He slowly turned the knob on Velma's office door and sauntered into the room.

His mouth lost the smirk it had carried for the past hour and fell open as the first barrage of words hit him.

"You Black bastard," Velma said, shocked at her own words. She didn't curse, but this man was enough to drive her to it. Justified, she immediately got over the shock of hearing such a phrase come from her mouth and continued without missing a beat. "I am the head of this agency now. I make all final decisions! Our relationship will not be like the one you had with the late William Ellis Colby. We are not buddies! Maybe he enjoyed hearing about all of your women and your sexual prowess, but I am not interested!"

She did not offer him a seat, and he did not dare take one without permission, not after seeing the rage on his employer's face. He stood staring at her. He was dumbfounded and angry with himself, for although this woman was reading him up one side and down the other, he still thought she was the most enchanting creature he had ever seen.

"The only time your black behind will interest me is when it is moving in the capacity for which it was hired here at The William E. Colby Agency. To create! In the Creative Department! The department that has been assigned to you!" she continued.

Bradley's eyes were glued to Velma's distorted face. Her eyes blazed, and the middle finger of her right hand was trying to punch a hole in the top of the beautiful white antique desk—that he hoped she would not leap across at him, but looked as if she might do so any moment.

"And if your black behind does not function in the capacity for which it was hired here, it is going to be pounding the streets in search of other employment," Velma went on.

"I've been with this company for twelve years." He dared to speak for the first time since entering the room.

"Well, if you don't get your butt in gear, your twelfth year will be your last!" she hissed at him.

"Look Vel." He smiled at her, his best come-on.

"My name is Miss Hannah!"

"Say, baby," he tried again.

"I said, my name is Miss Hannah! Not Vel! Not baby! Do you understand me?"

"All right, Miss Hannah. I don't have lots of women. Honest. Now if that's what's bothering you... Remember, I wanted you to be my woman when we first met long before all this." His eyes surveyed the exquisitely furnished office. "I tried." He smiled cockily at her. "Now if you've changed your mind..." He held out his arms as if ready to enfold her in them.

"Why you egotistical, arrogant..." she left the sentence dangling for lack of a civil word to call this conceited man. "This conversation is over. Get your sorry ass to work, Mr. Morris! If I don't see an improvement in your department, and soon, I'm going to see that overly-inflated head of yours lead the rest of your carcass out onto Broadwalk Avenue for the last time."

Bradley thought of something else to say but immediately thought better of the idea. The woman was for real. The honky loving... She was too good for him. Had waited and schemed until she got into "the "man's" office, then had run off with him like some cold hearted...

Whatever she had done to the poor bastard had worked. She became an instant millionaire—after the man's heart gave out, probably trying to keep up with her sexual demands. Slept her way from the secretarial pool—the lowest rung of the ladder, next to maintenance—all the way to the top floor.

Sitting here in her intimidating office. Red of all colors. She had the whole office redecorated after the man died. She had painted the walls with William Colby's blood and was now trying to use his for touch up.

Yes, the lady had the upper hand all right. Half of the agency was hers now. And worst of all, she was his boss and was threatening to fire him. Him. Bradley Morris, the best creative director the agency ever had. The best! She would never find a replacement for him. Not in a million years.

Yes, he and William Colby had a good relationship—on the surface, anyway. And, yes, he had told Colby, from time to time, about the women he dated, but he did not know the man was going to tell his woman. Pillow talk. Hell, he didn't expect to have the same kind of relationship with her. After all, she was a woman.

"Move!" Velma's voice thundered through his thoughts.

He did.

This time, Bradley did not stroll down the hallway. He almost ran the distance to the stairs (the elevators were too slow), down the stairs to the next floor, and down the hallway to his office—his face, a mask of terror.

Bradley Morris went hurriedly through his department, surveyed the somewhat relaxed atmosphere in the various departments, and began barking orders to his subordinates.

CHAPTER 9

When Bradley Morris graduated from college fifteen years earlier, he had high hopes. He was a darned good artist, and he knew it. He had even put a couple of his teachers to shame. One, he had hated: Herbert Dobbs. The man had about as much business teaching art as Bradley would have teaching a foreign language.

Bradley had to chuckle whenever he thought about the time Dobbs brought in a painting of his wife to show the class. He had worked on it for a couple of months. His wife had posed for it in the evenings after Dobbs got home from the university. Dobbs had proudly displayed his masterpiece to the class. Then he told them that his wife would be in before the period was over to stand beside the painting, so they could compare the work to the live model.

Bradley thought the portrait looked rather amateurish. The lighting source wasn't well directed, and the pallet was overused, among a few other flaws.

When Mrs. Dobbs appeared, Bradley let his instructor have it, pointing out detail after detail that could have improved the painting. He even offered to make some touch ups on the painting right there before the entire class. Dobbs had been furious, Bradley had gloated, and his grades had plummeted.

"Well, what I said was nothing but the truth," Bradley told a classmate after receiving his low grade in Dobbs' class.

"Yeah," said the classmate, "but the next time you criticize Dobbs, make sure you're talking to somebody else and his wife isn't around."

"I always speak my mind," Bradley countered.

"Well, you'd better learn to sit on it," his classmate advised.

Bradley never learned to sit on it.

He and Dobbs did reach an understanding, however, and his grades rose enough to enable him to graduate at the top of his class. Third, to be exact. Of course, he thought he should have been number one and wasted no time trying to convince the school officials that they should have thought so, too. He was not successful, however, so he reluctantly accepted third place status.

Bradley had chosen the school in the mid-west upon the recommendation of his high school art teacher. "It's the best," his instructor said.

Bradley found the school to be all his teacher promised. It had a challenging curriculum, the best teachers—except for Dobbs. Bradley did not know how that dumb klutz had gotten through the door. There seemed to always be at least one in every bunch of anything worthwhile. That was just the way it was—until some great somebody changed the whole structure of things.

On graduation day, Bradley's family had come up from Arkansas: his mother, his father, and his two sisters. They watched Bradley receive his piece of sheepskin. Then they all tried desperately to talk him into coming back home.

"For what?" Bradley asked.

"Because that's home," his father said.

"So you can give back to your community," his mother said.

"Yeah. Can't you just see the kids in our community lining up to take art lessons?" Bradley said.

As usual, Bradley won the argument showing his family where he could make more money in the mid-west.

And now that he had his degree, it would be a cinch. He would make so much money, he would be able to send some home to help out from time to time.

That did it.

"That sounds real good," said Alicia, one of his sisters.

"Real good," agreed Justine, his other sister.

So Bradley, with degree in hand and all the confidence in the world, set out to paint the world and become an instant millionaire.

About a year and a half after graduating from college, he thought he had accomplished the first part of his dream. He had traveled extensively and painted everything he thought at least half the country (that was surely waiting for his masterpieces to grace the walls of their homes) would want.

He sold a few pieces here and there. Finally, he talked one of his many conquests, a rich widow, into sponsoring a few shows for him that brought in a little money. She later took him to south-central Europe where he painted the Alps; to Paris where he painted the Eiffel Tower and a few other pieces; then on to the Palace of Versailles in Versailles, France where he painted the Hall of Mirrors: his masterpieces—or, at least, he thought they were. His lady friend took the Hall of Mirrors, and he sold the Eiffel Tower for a fraction of what he knew it was worth.

He placed his paintings in banks and other places that sold them on consignment. Every now and then, a few pieces were sold. But most of this great artist's masterpieces graced his own walls. Those he did not have room for on the walls were stacked in closets and behind his sofa. Some, he gave away as gifts.

Bradley soon had to face reality. If he was going to keep a roof over his head, fill the hole in his stomach, and keep his love life going, he had to find a job. It was either that or be a kept man. He did not like the latter alternative.

After a lengthy period of searching, Bradley saw the Colby Agency's ad for an assistant creative director. He applied for the job. William Colby and the chief creative director liked him and loved his work, so he was hired on the spot.

Three years later, the chief creative director set his sights on something bigger and left the agency. Bradley stepped into the vacancy, and he had been helping to build the William E. Colby Agency ever since.

As for the women in his life, Bradley never had a problem. His six feet, chocolate brown, one hundred and ninety pound frame got them. His intelligence kept them. He was sexy and irresistible. He knew it, and he flaunted it. Women loved him, and he lapped up their attention. He had always been able to outtalk any woman. He won every argument and had the women apologizing to him even when he was as wrong as two left shoes.

Marriage, he could do without. Maybe someday, but no time soon. Why should he? He was having too much fun being a bachelor. He had never been turned down by any woman in his life until... He still could not believe it.

One morning, Bradley's secretary called in sick. Bradley was beside himself, because he needed a lot of paper work done that day. He called down to personnel, and they sent up a girl. He was busy at his desk when she arrived. Bradley heard the knock on his private office door.

"Come in," he said without looking up.

"Mr. Morris?" his visitor asked as she stepped into the room, closing the door quietly behind her.

"Yes," Bradley said. His head was still buried in the work before him, and there was irritation in his voice—not at the girl but at the disorder in his office and the feeling that the entire day would be hopeless. Utterly. Of all times for his secretary to get sick.

"I'm Miss Hannah from personnel," the woman said.

Bradley finally looked up, and his gut tightened at what he saw. He simply stared at the woman. What had she said her name was?

"I'm substituting for your secretary today," the woman continued.

"Yes," Bradley finally managed to say. He felt like a fool. He was gawking at the woman. He felt the blood rush to his face, and he wondered just what he looked like to the magnificent creature that stood before him. Talking about lighting up a canvass, this woman would make a canvass glow with a ten-mile radius.

His imaginary brush began at the top with the naturally-curly, dark brown, hair—cut and styled to frame a face with lines he would never tire of creating on canvass, the kind of lines about which an artist dreamed. His brush moved on to outline that smooth, olive colored, majestic piece of art that housed a pair of the biggest, brownest, most captivating eyes he had ever seen. Beneath those eyes sat a perky nose that his brush captured in a second, on its way to a pair of lips that would take the rest of the day to duplicate—and it still would not do those lips justice. She was tall, about four inches shorter than he; her breasts were not big but not small either. He jutted them just the right amount on his imaginary canvass. The waistline dipped into place, then he stroked on down to slightly bowed hips. (God, he loved women with bowed hips. They looked so, so...) He had to finish the portrait. But, no, he had to stop. The legs were hidden behind the other side of his desk. He would have to finish this true masterpiece later.

Bradley rose and came awkwardly around the desk. This woman was a goddess. She had to be the most gorgeous female alive, or his eyes were doing a darn good job of playing tricks on him.

Get a grip, man, he thought. What was wrong with him? Was he losing control over a woman? He had seen many beautiful women, had dated them, had... He did not even know who this woman was.

"I, uh, didn't get the name, uh...?"

"Miss Hannah. Velma Hannah." she said.

"Yes, well, Miss Hannah... uh... let's go into the next room, shall we?" He waved a hand indicating that they go into the outer office. He followed her to the door, his eyes glued to the slight swaying of her hips. Those hips. He shook his head as if to awaken his senses. He had to get control of himself. She was just a woman. He caught up to her and opened the door. They went into the next room.

"This is where you will work, Miss Hannah. May I call you Velma?" he continued as he indicated his secretary's desk.

"Miss Hannah, please."

"Then Miss Hannah it is. Well, Miss Hannah, I'm afraid this is going to be a busy day for you. This is a hectic time in my department. Maybe that's why my secretary is ill. I've worked her awfully hard for the past few days." He smiled at her and pulled out the chair behind the desk for her to sit.

Velma smiled back as she lowered herself into the chair, and Bradley's heart caught in his throat. Her eyes lit up, prompting soft smile lines to appear on the sides of them, and her nose actually seemed to twinkle. He would have a wonderful time painting that smile and all the irresistible innuendoes it triggered—and that mouthful of pearly whites.

"I'm sure I can manage, Mr. Morris. Where do I begin?"

"I'll show you," he managed to say, almost strangling on the words. He swallowed hard. What in the world was wrong with him? "Are you a temporary?" he continued.

"No, I work here. In personnel. I wasn't too busy today, so they sent me up instead of calling an agency."

"I see."

Bradley managed to show Velma what needed to be done in spite of the fact that he felt flushed. In fact, he felt hot all over—a feeling that devastated him, a feeling he had never experienced before.

***

Bradley had not done much work that morning. After briefing Velma on what he needed done, he went back into his office, closed the door, and sat staring at the wall that separated the two rooms for an hour or so— through the wall, in his mind's eyes, at the woman in the next room.

He thought about asking her to lunch. He certainly could not take her downstairs to the company dining room, although their presence there might appear to be perfectly natural. But he did not know the woman, her friends, if she was having an affair with someone at the agency, or if she was married. No, he guessed not. She said her name was Miss Hannah.

Good try, Bradley thought. Then he admitted to himself that he could not take the woman to lunch downstairs or anywhere else, because he did not trust himself with her even in a crowded restaurant. He would have been a blundering idiot.

No woman had ever put Bradley Morris to such a disadvantage. He did not know how to handle this strange situation. So at eleven-thirty, Bradley brushed past his secretary's desk where Velma sat engrossed in work, and mumbled that he was going to lunch.

"All right, Mr. Morris. Have a good one," she said without looking up at him.

Bradley went to a little Italian restaurant around the corner for lunch, as did most of the executives from the agency from time to time. It was an atmospheric place with excellent food and delectable drinks.

Velma stopped working just long enough to eat a sandwich and drink a bottle of juice that she had brought from home.

Bradley picked at his food, leaving most of it on his plate, but managed to down three martinis. He arrived back at the office feeling much better about himself and his abilities.

Toward the end of the day, he had a Scotch and water from his private stock in his office. Then, his nerves in tip-top condition, or so he thought, he went out into the front office to do what he had wanted to do all day. He approached Velma who was still hard at work at his secretary's desk.

"Uh, Miss Hannah, how would you like to meet me around the corner after work for a cocktail?"

"No, thank you, Mr. Morris," she said without even glancing up at him.

There was a moment of silence as Bradley let her refusal sink in. "All right, then," he said. "If you're busy tonight, how about another evening?"

She looked up, and her eyes told him even before she spoke that she was not interested. "I'm not busy, Mr. Morris. I simply don't want to have a drink with you."

"I see. Okay." Bradley turned without another word, went back into his office, and closed the door.

He felt like a complete idiot. He sat for a long while in stunned silence, his thoughts racing. The woman had actually turned him down flat. A secretary, of all people. A mere...nobody. He had never... How could he ever face her again? But he had to go check on some of his staff. He had to go past her in order to get out of the office.

Maybe she'll have to go pee or something, he thought.

Thirty minutes later, she still had not left the office. Bradley could not wait any longer. He had work to do. He got up, walked to the door of his private office—where he lingered a few seconds—then opened the door and walked out into his secretary's office. He went through the office without even a glance in Velma's direction.

Out of the corner of her eye, Velma watched the presumptuous, arrogant man leave the office. She had heard about the handsome, dynamic chief creative director, and she wasn't about to become another of his victims. He was known for playing with his conquests for a little while then dumping them. Little did he know, even if she were interested (and she might be if he didn't have such a bad reputation) she would not fit into his game plan.

Just what I need, another man who can't cope, she thought.

She dismissed Bradley Morris from her mind and went back to work.

After his third drink, Bradley lost count. After making his rounds among his staff, he had gone back to the little restaurant where he had lunch and literally tried to drown his disappointment. He waited until well after quitting time before going back to the office. When he did, Velma Hannah was gone. The work was finished, and his secretary's desk had been cleared.

"Good," he said out loud. *I couldn't face her again, not today anyway,* he thought. A secretary had turned him down. He must have been losing his touch.

Velma Hannah was a good worker. She had proven herself to be fast, competent, and most efficient. But Bradley found himself hoping his secretary would be back in the office the next day. If she called in sick again, he hoped Miss Hannah would not be sent up to fill in for her. But how could he prevent that possibility? He couldn't say the woman was incompetent, although after what had just gone down between them… No, that wasn't his style. And they surely knew the woman's qualifications downstairs.

Bradley's secretary did return to work the next day. She said she was feeling much better. But Bradley was not successful in his attempts to get Velma Hannah, nor the events of the day before, out of his mind.

He did not see Velma again until she became William Colby's personal assistant. He could not have avoided her then if he had wanted to, for he was always in and out of the top man's office. He merely greeted her curtly whenever he went in to see William. She returned his curt greeting and always appeared to be busy.

Bradley did not approach her about going out with him again. He decided that she either hated men, or she was a lesbian.

Bradley and William Colby lunched together quite often. They talked candidly with each other, but the man never mentioned women except his wife and daughter. William told him about the problems he was having with his wife, that they were estranged—living in the same house, but apart as husband and wife.

Bradley never dreamed, never had any reason to believe, there was anything going on between Colby and his new assistant.

Then the tongues began to wag.

When the buzz reached Bradley's ears, he could not believe it. He was shocked, and then he was furious. He wanted to do something bad to both of them—her for choosing a White man over him, and Colby for having the gall to go after what he wanted in spite of all the odds.

After it was out in the open, the man had the audacity to talk with Bradley about it—for lack of anybody else to dump his troubles on, Bradley assumed. All his uppity White friends had probably dumped him. Or maybe he felt safe talking to an African-American man about his African-American woman. Or maybe he just wanted to see how Bradley would feel about the situation. And Bradley had to appear to be impartial, when he really felt like going upside the man's head. But this was his employer. This was the man who kept clothes on his back, food in his stomach, money in his pocket, and more women than ever now in his love nest—for he was still trying to prove to himself that Velma Hannah meant nothing to him.

No, he could not do anything to jeopardize his job, so he would have to settle for hating them. He listened to the man talk about the new woman in his life. He told him how wonderful and warm she was, how much he loved her, how he had never loved so completely before, how lucky he was to have a woman like Velma Hannah in his life, how she made him feel so clean and decent.

Clean and decent. How the man had the nerve to utter the words, Bradley would never understand. But he listened, smiled in the man's face, and then cursed him behind his back. He let Velma know his feelings in subtle ways, also. After all, she was sleeping with "the man," so he had to be careful. Pillow talk could be lethal sometimes.

Bradley continued to tell himself that his hatred for Velma Hannah was the reason his stomach tied itself in knots every time he saw her.

Now, he had to answer to the woman.

After work that day, he got into his Mercedes-Benz and drove straight home. The encounter with Velma at the meeting that morning filled his thoughts.

He broke a dinner date and ate a lonely T. V. Dinner while watching the evening news. He went to bed early but could not sleep. Instead, he tossed and turned most of the night, thinking about Velma Hannah.

CHAPTER 10

Callie sat in Kuplins, one of the most prestigious and expensive restaurants in Baltonville.

She wore a white, brocade and sequined, formfitting dress that dipped quite low in the front. She thought the dress enhanced her well-rounded, shapely figure like no other garment ever had. On her fingers were pearls, diamonds, and a few colorful stones. About her neck was a diamond necklace. Her hair was swept up on top of her head in the style she now referred to as her "dress up hairdo."

She looked radiant. She felt even better than that. She felt wonderful. She felt... rich. Yes, that was it. She felt like the rich lady she had recently become.

Callie looked about the restaurant admiring the décor. "Some place," she whispered to herself.

A fancily dressed waiter—tails and all—approached her table. "Is Madam ready to order?" he asked.

"Yes, Madam is," Callie said in her most sophisticated voice. "I'll have the lobster Newburg, please." She had looked at all the fancy stuff on the menu, and had decided the lobster Newburg looked about the safest.

"Very good, Madam. An excellent choice. What kind of dressing would you like on your salad?"

"Vinegar and oil," Callie said.

"Very good," the waiter said. He took her menu and left the table.

"Fancy, fancy," Callie whispered to herself. *They even call you madam*, she thought.

In a moment, the man, who had told her earlier that he was the wine steward, approached her table. He carried a bottle of imported (or so he said) wine, wrapped in a napkin, in one hand and a fancy cooler in the other.

He had assisted Callie in the selection of her bottle of wine, telling her all about the taste and the year. Oh, he had made a big to-do over the year. Callie had learned something: rich folks might throw their mothers and fathers away when they got old but a bottle of wine, they'd hang onto forever. And just like antique furniture, the older the wine, the more expensive it was. And, of course, it was imported.

From where? Callie thought. But if rich folks liked imported wine, so would she since she was of that class of people now.

The Colby family had not been wine drinkers. At Christmas time, they would buy champagne, and Callie had drunk some of that, but she wasn't sure if that was imported or not. The Colbys had loved their dry martinis (that tasted like leftover dishwater to Callie). Except for the girl. Now Sonya and her friends would drink anything, even Callie's Thunderbird if she left a bottle where it could be found.

The slut, Callie thought as her hatred for the girl soared within her. That gal would probably be a drunk, too, soon.

Callie would have to remember to throw her cheap wine away when she returned to the house. She would replace it with the best money could buy.

The man set the freestanding cooler beside the table. He then poured a few drops of wine into Callie's glass. Callie looked at the glass then up at the man, and there was no doubt in her mind that he had taken complete leave of his senses. He was standing at attention, like the penguin he looked like, staring at her as if he expected her to do something with that smidgen of wine. It wasn't enough to even wet her throat.

After a moment of deliberation, Callie decided she had to do something before the man got a crook in his neck.

She guessed she would just drink it, then she would tell him to set the bottle down, and she would pour her own wine if he didn't know how to fill a glass.

Callie glanced about the room to see if others were watching what was happening at her table. She was shocked to see the same ritual going on at another table across the room.

Well, I'll be darned. Just like rinsing after brushing your teeth except you don't spit it out, Callie thought.

When in Rome... Callie delicately picked up her glass, made sure she was holding it properly—pinkie showing and all—sniffed it, then poured some of the wine into her mouth. All her great expectations of the expensive liquid died on the spot. That was the worst, god-awful, tasting stuff.

But she couldn't let the people here in this highfalutin place know she had never tasted an expensive wine before, now could she? She proceeded to duplicate the action she thought she had seen from across the room. She rinsed her mouth, threw back her head, gargled, swished the liquid around her mouth again, and then swallowed.

Callie looked up at the wine steward who reeled and looked as if he was about to faint, his eyes darting about the restaurant as if he was trying to find something to crawl under. Callie nodded her head (as she had seen the man across the room do). The waiter filled her glass so fast some of the liquid spilled over onto the tablecloth. Without taking time to wipe up the mess he had made, the man threw the bottle into the cooler, and literally raced from the table.

"Well, what's the matter with him?" Callie said to herself as she wiped at the spilled wine with her napkin. *Guess he has more glasses to fill with this nasty-tasting mess,* she thought.

Yes, Callie Foster was learning the ways of the rich and famous. As long as things didn't get too way out, she would give them a shot. She was still confused about the wine bit, though. She guessed she had been a little loud with her gargle. She hadn't heard the man at the other table when he gargled. Or maybe he hadn't. But he had tilted back his head, so what else could he have been doing?

Anyway, why all the fuss?

Oh, well, she would just sit, look beautiful, and daintily sip her wine until her lobster Newburg arrived. Maybe she would even acquire a taste for the stuff.

Callie had never eaten lobster before. She had read on the menu that the Newburg was made with chopped lobster. *Thank God*, she thought. She wouldn't know how to eat the darned thing. Why couldn't they just fry up a mess of catfish and be done with it?

Callie got out of the cab in front of a house a block down the street from the Colby estate. She did not want to draw suspicion to herself, and if she did, she did not want to do so at the Colby place. She waved the cab driver on, after giving the poor slob a nice tip, of course (civil servant that he was), and walked slowly toward the big rambling structure that loomed before her. She stopped at the gate pretending to get her keys out of her handbag.

When the taxi was far enough down the street, she turned, walked back to the sidewalk, and headed hurriedly for the Colby residence. A few minutes later, she let herself in through the servants' entrance. That was the only thing she disliked about her new existence—she was still coming into the Colby house like a servant.

Past history, Callie thought. Callie Foster would never be in a position of servitude to anybody ever again.

She had been living in the Colby house for a few months now. She had stashed away a substantial sum of money and was continually adding to it as she slowly cleaned out the place of all its valuables.

Callie had been thinking about her next move and decided that, when she left the Colby estate, she would make her home in Switzerland. Go skiing and do all that other stuff people with money did. Callie had never been on a pair of skis in her life, but she was game. Yes, she was going to live the good life. She had what it took now—money.

The girl was a fool to leave all this, she thought.

But Callie was grateful to the little wench. Of course, the jewels had been locked in the safe. Safe from possible theft, right? Maybe safe from the ordinary thief. As Callie's husband once told her, she was a smart woman.

She wondered where Walter was now and when he had stopped looking for her, if he had ever divorced her and married again. What kind of woman? Could she cook? *He probably looks like a fat cow about now*, Callie thought.

Callie froze as she opened the door from the back hallway. The lights were on in the living room. She had not noticed them from the outside. She had been too engrossed in her thoughts, she guessed. Then she heard someone moving about upstairs. She moved quickly back into the hallway and closed the door behind her leaving a crack to peek through. What was going on? Who in the world was in her house this time of night?

In a few minutes, she heard footsteps descending the stairs. But more than one set. It sounded like two people.

"Why didn't you come before now, Mr. Forrister?" a male voice asked.

"Because the girl just called me. Today, in fact, and I came over as soon as I could," Maurice Forrister said.

"It's that lawyer," Callie whispered to herself. And the police? she wondered.

"It looks like a professional job," the other voice said.

"I should have come sooner," Maurice said.

"I'll bring some of my men out tomorrow. We'll see what we can do," the other man said.

"Thank you, Chief. I'll meet you here. I'll call you tomorrow morning. In the meantime, I'll report this to the insurance company."

"It is the police," Callie whispered to herself.

The two men reached the front door, and Maurice Forrister turned around to survey the house once more before leaving.

Callie stared in disbelief. Hanging over Forrister's arm was a stack of fur pieces. She saw the full-length mink, the short white ermine, at least one of the stoles, and the tails of the fox boa dangling about his legs. "He's taking my furs," she whispered to herself.

Forrister clicked the light switch beside the door, and the room was engulfed in darkness. Callie heard the front door slam and locks turning. She waited a few moments then hurried through the living room and up the stairs to the second floor. She raced to the bedroom that she now occupied and rushed over to the wall safe. She took down the picture. In a few moments, she had the safe open. She looked inside.

"Empty. All my jewels. Gone! They're all gone!" she moaned.

She hurried into the clothes closet and searched rapidly through it. "All my furs," she gasped. "He took every one of them. I only have what I'm wearing."

Callie looked at the rings on her fingers then touched the necklace around her neck. She pulled the stole from about her shoulders and hugged it to her. Then she slumped to the floor and cried.

Callie slept downstairs in the servants' quarters that night. She would have to lie low until this thing about the theft blew over. She was smart, but the girl had outsmarted her this time. The heifer had finally thought to call the lawyer and have her mother's valuables picked up.

Callie should have anticipated such a move. She should have sold all the jewels and the furs.

All that money. Gone, she thought. She could have had so much more. She could have bought more jewelry later.

No, the girl was not as dumb as Callie thought.

Sure enough, they came the next day: the lawyer, the police chief and some of his men, and the insurance man.

Callie stood at the door in the back hallway listening.

"This way, gentlemen," she heard the lawyer say.

Forrister led the men up the stairs to the second floor.

Callie listened as best she could from downstairs, but she couldn't hear anything but a lot of walking around and muffled voices. One thing she was sure of though: Callie Foster was not a suspect in this crime. She smiled to herself. She would not worry about what she could have had. She was thankful for what she did have.

Some of that jewelry was expensive, and she had gotten paid handsomely for it. If she invested wisely, she could probably live comfortably for the rest of her life. And until she decided to make her move, she always had access to other valuables in the house. The place was loaded with all kinds of goodies.

Her man would take anything and pay top dollar for it. She wondered to whom he sold all that hot stuff. She knew there were people who would buy most anything no matter how hot, and she was sure the fence was making a handsome profit.

Sonya would not even miss the items. In fact, she probably didn't even know what was in the house. *That girl couldn't care less*, Callie thought.

She doubted if Sonya ever went into the kitchen. Her meals were always prepared for her and served in the dining room, or in bed. That was one worthless child. But Callie guessed that was another advantage of having money. People could be as lazy as they wanted to be when they had the green stuff and other people working for them.

Callie had to work faster than she planned. She made a mental note to take stock of all the items in the house she could pawn as soon as the men upstairs left.

A short while later, Callie heard them coming down the stairs. She peeked out through her crack in the back hallway door. There were about six of them, and Maurice Forrister was leading the pack.

"Check all the doors and windows," the chief said.

The men spread out and went through the downstairs checking every possible entry into the house.

"It didn't look like a forced entry," Callie heard the chief say. "Every door seems in tack, unless I missed something," he went on. "I'd say the person used keys or is an expert at picking locks."

"If he picked that safe upstairs, he is an expert," Forrister added.

Callie smiled. Yes, she was an expert all right—an expert at keeping her eyes and ears open.

"I don't' think they came through the front door. Both of the locks were still in place, and they are the best money can buy. It would have taken an awfully long time to pick them," one of the other men said.

"They had all the time in the world. There's no one living here now, you know. And maybe they know that, too. Crooks are smart. They could have been watching the place for months," Forrister offered.

"Just waiting for the right time," another man said.

"All the doors have especially good locks, except maybe the servants' entrance. It has a dead bolt, but not one of the best," the chief said.

They were all standing at the bottom of the stairs now.

"We'll check it out. Which way?" Callie heard another man say.

"Through there," Forrister said.

"They're coming in here," Callie whispered. Her mind began to race wildly. She had to hide. But where? In her room, of course. She tiptoed quickly back into her old room, grabbed the fur stole off the bed and the jewelry off the old beat up dresser, and scurried, with her possessions, under the bed.

She heard footsteps pass her bedroom door, going to the servants' entrance. In a few moments, they were back. They stopped just outside the door. Then Callie heard the door open and saw two pairs of feet enter the room. She stopped breathing for the few moments they stood there.

"They wouldn't want anything from in here," one of the men said. "Must be part of the servants' quarters."

"Right," the other one said. He chuckled. "We get paid peanuts to protect these people with their big fancy homes, cars, jewelry, furs, and servants. That's what we are, too, man: part of the domestic staff. But we don't just work for one family. We work for all of them. We're even servants to the servants."

"Yeah. It's a hell of a life," the other man said. "Let's get out of here."

"Right."

They left the room, closing the door behind them, and went on down the hallway.

Callie heard another door open. They must have been checking all the rooms. Maybe they thought the burglar was still there. Callie chuckled softly.

Well, in a way, I guess she is at that, she thought.

Callie could not hear a word that was being said now, so she took her chances and came out from under the bed, leaving the fur piece and the jewelry. She stood at the door of the room until she heard the men go back out into the living room area, and then she opened the door a crack and looked out into the hallway. The coast was clear. She crept back to the hallway door to listen.

"I'll have it replaced later today," Forrister was saying.

"That's a good idea," the chief said.

"He's going to have the lock changed," Callie whispered.

How would she get in and out of the house? She couldn't. What was she going to do? What else could she do but get out?

Well, it was fun while it lasted, she thought.

Callie stood, a look of dread on her face. She did not have enough time to do what she had to do. She felt trapped. She had to hurry.

In a few moments, Callie heard the front door close and the locks slide into place. "They're gone," she said to herself. She raced back into her old room, retrieved the fur stole and the jewelry from under the bed, then hurried through the house and up the stairs to the bedroom she had grown to love. She went straight to the closet and began pulling down pieces of luggage from a top shelf.

"At least I've got a beautiful set of luggage," she said to herself as she began pulling dresses, skirts, blouses, blazers, slacks, and negligee sets off racks. "And lots of clothes," she continued. "I'd better not wear the jewelry and the stole. I'll pack them nice and neat."

Callie stuffed the five-piece set of luggage to capacity and took it, one heavy piece at a time, downstairs and out the back door. She hid the luggage between the shrubbery and the fence in the backyard. Then she went to work in the kitchen and dining room. She stuffed all the silver, crystal and other small items she thought she could sell into bags and hid them in the backyard along with the luggage.

Callie went back upstairs and chose a dress, she could not fit into the luggage, to wear. She decided to take a bath. Her last bath in that sunken tub with all the gadgets that made her feel like a queen.

Afterwards, she splashed herself with extravagant perfume and hurriedly got dressed.

She went back into the closet and pulled an armload of handbags from a shelf, chose one to take, put the items she needed inside, and then stuffed the others with perfume and other items from the well-stocked vanity. She rushed from the room and down the hallway to Sonya's room. She found an odd piece of luggage in the closet and stuffed the handbags into it. Then she hurried down the stairs and out the back door with it.

Callie had her plan all laid. She would take the luggage, several pieces at a time, to a motel where she would stay until she had gotten rid of all the loot, and then she would leave the country for good. A simple matter. She would take two pieces now and the rest after dark.

She wished she could think of a way to get rid of the priceless antique furniture Claire Colby had doted on for years. It was all over the house and would bring her a small fortune.

But I won't dwell on that. I'm doing just fine for myself, Callie thought.

Maybe a few of the small paintings, though.

"No one has ever pushed Callie Foster into a corner yet, and no one ever will," Callie told herself.

CHAPTER 11

Callie's plan worked beautifully. She checked into a motel in the middle class section of Baltonville under the assumed name of Nancy Clemons. During the next week, she managed to get rid of all the silver and most of the other items she had taken from the Colby house. Her man, the fence, seemed awfully glad to get his hands on whatever she could bring him. She had a feeling he was ripping her off, but she was ripping somebody else off, too, she guessed, so she would not complain. She carried the expensive items to the shop in some of the suitcases she emptied especially for this operation.

On the night before she was to leave town, Callie packed her clothes and confirmed her reservation at the airport. She was leaving the next day on TWA flight number seven eighty-four. She would arrive in Chicago that evening where she would board her flight to London and from there her Swissair flight.

Callie's fence had put her in touch with a man who supplied her with a forged passport in her new name and who also showed her how to open a Swiss bank account. Callie Foster, aka Nancy Clemons, was set. She was home free. Callie Foster had finally been liberated.

"Nothing can stop me now," she told herself.

She thought of Joe and their good-byes the night before. She had waited until the last minute to tell him she was leaving town and still had not told him she was leaving the country—and for good. Instead she said she was going to Chicago. Well, in a way, that was true.

"I'll call you when I get there," she lied.

"All right," he said.

Callie knew Joe had not believed her from the way he was talking when he left, and she wondered why she had even bothered to tell the lie.

Callie tried on her beautiful, expensive jewelry one last time on the eve of her scheduled departure from Baltonville. "Exquisite," she said as she smiled at her reflection in the mirror. "Callie, you're going to give those Swiss men hell."

Then she re-packed the precious gems and went to bed, her mind full of the new, exciting life that awaited her.

Callie went to the airport early the next day. With all the new regulations now, she wanted to make sure she did not have any problems. She would be in another country soon. *Good-bye good old U. S. of A. You've been extremely good to me, but I've got to leave you now*, she thought.

Callie checked her luggage through and thanked God that she did not beep when she went through the security gate. She then went on to her departing gate and took a seat to wait the hour and a half until boarding time.

She had the latest Dumàs novel that she was planning to read—before all the mess back at the house broke loose—to keep her occupied. One reviewer had branded the new author a female James Patterson. Well, she would see for herself if the woman could write.

She pulled *Facades* out of her carry-on and began to read.

"May I have your attention, please?" the heavy accented female voice came over the intercom.

Callie looked up from her reading.

"Flight seven eighty-four to Chicago will be delayed for approximately three hours due to circumstances beyond our control," the voice went on. "We hope this will not inconvenience those of you traveling to Chicago with us too much. We shall keep you updated. Thank you for your patience."

"What?" Callie said.

"It's a shame, ain't it? They're always doing something to upset your schedule. I've got to get home," an elderly, gray haired woman sitting to Callie's right said.

"I know that's the truth," Callie said. "I can't just sit here."

"What else can we do?" the woman asked.

"I don't know, but I've got a million things I could be doing."

"Well, if you want to go take care of some of your business, I would be more than happy to watch your carry-on for you."

"Would you?" Callie asked.

"Of course. You run along. Your bag and I will be sitting right here when you get back."

"That's really kind of you. I can't thank you enough." Callie offered the woman her hand. "I'm Cal, uh, Nancy Clemons."

"Nice to meet you Ms. Nancy Clemons. I'm Mrs. Mary Elizabeth Richardson," the woman said shaking Callie's hand.

"See you in a little while, Mrs. Richardson."

"Nice lady." Callie chuckled to herself as she hurried back through the airport.

Callie thought, since she was being delayed, she might as well go see her fence one last time. She had left a few small items from the Colby house, that she had not had time to deliver, in her motel room. In three hours, she could go get them, deliver them to her fence, and make it back to the airport in time to catch her flight. She would just tell the manager she had forgotten something. He would let her back into the room.

Callie's visit to her fence proved to be a fruitful one—just like all the others had been. The cab driver got her there in record time. She told him she was in a hurry, and he had complied. Callie was elated that she had done so well. She never knew making money could be so easy.

She checked her watch and decided she had time to shop a bit since she was already in the downtown area. She would leave some of her newfound wealth in the town that had been so good to her. She would have one last fling at D'Ambara's, one of the most exclusive department stores in Baltonville.

Her purchase would have to be something small but exquisite, of course. What would fit that description more than a nice piece of jewelry? A black pearl ring similar to the one that had been among the late Claire Gene Colby's jewels—that that fat clown of a lawyer had taken. Something Callie had always wanted but had been forced to admire from afar—until now.

In her elated state of mind, Callie lost track of the time. She missed her plane.

Mrs. Mary Elizabeth Richardson had deliberated with herself about what to do with Nancy Clemons' bag. She decided she would take the bag on the plane with her. Surely Ms. Clemons would make it back to the airport before they departed. The planes always sat on the ground a few minutes before taking off after boarding. If Ms. Clemons didn't make it, she would just leave the bag at the baggage claim department in Chicago. She could pick it up there.

Her arthritic knees were hurting. That meant it was going to storm. Mrs. Richardson hoped her plane could get out of town before it started.

Callie Foster, alias Nancy Clemons, could have kicked herself for missing her flight. She was now booked on an eleven p.m. flight that would take her into Chicago, where she would have to sit for four more hours before boarding her connecting flight. She had messed up royally. But, she could live with it. She would console herself by thinking about the good life she was about to embark upon in Switzerland—with her newfound wealth, of course.

She had checked at the ticket counter, and Mrs. Richardson had not left her carry-on there. She would check again when she got to Chicago.

The old girl appeared to be an honest person, but you could never tell, Callie thought. Mrs. Richardson could be a crook just like anybody else. Some weirdo dressed up like an old woman. They came in all shapes and sizes. But, then, she was one to talk, wasn't she?

Well what goes around comes around, she thought. So she wouldn't worry about it. There was nothing of importance in the carry-on anyway. Just the ordinary everyday stuff.

She just hoped her other luggage would be waiting for her when she arrived at her final destination. She had plenty of money in her Swiss bank account, but she would hate to lose all of her fancy new clothes and the few jewels she had managed to save from the clutches of that meddling lawyer.

Callie sat waiting for her flight to leave when something a newscaster said on the television up in the corner of the waiting area caught her attention. She looked up from her reading.

"...an update on the plane crash in Chicago," the newscaster was saying.

Plane crash? Callie thought. *What a story to be broadcasting at an airport.*

"The police are looking for a Nancy Clemons," the newscaster continued.

Callie froze.

"...who was booked on that flight but apparently was not aboard the aircraft," the newscaster went on. "Luggage belonging to Ms. Clemons was recovered from the wreckage."

Callie stood.

"All passengers and crew members aboard the aircraft were killed. The search for bodies continues, and the next of kin are being contacted. We now return to our regularly scheduled programming," the newscaster said, ending the news brief.

Callie picked up her handbag and hurried through the terminal. Her mind raced. Plane crash. All killed. And the police were looking for her? *When they put two and two together with that jewelry in my luggage, the hunt's on*, she thought

"Good Lord!" she almost screamed, and then covered her mouth with her hand, looking about, hoping no one had heard her. "They might think I sabotaged the plane," she whispered to herself. Callie was petrified. She picked up speed.

She found an exit and went swiftly through it. It was storming, and she didn't even have an umbrella. When had the storm come up? It had been so nice outside when she returned to the airport.

She hurried to the front of the line of the many cabs waiting outside the terminal. The driver opened the back door, and she got into the car. He closed the door and went around to the driver's side.

"Where to, lady?" he asked as he pulled the car away from the curb.

Where was she going? Callie really did not know. She hadn't even had time to think about that.

"Where to, lady?" the cab driver asked again, his voice louder this time.

"Downtown," Callie said. *I'll take a bus back*, she thought.

Back where? Where else? She would hide out at the house. They did not suspect Callie Foster. They wanted Nancy Clemons. Well, she would do away with Nancy Clemons forever. She would become herself again. After things blew over, she would find an apartment in a nice part of town and get on with her life. She would spend her money wisely—a little at a time, so as not to draw attention to herself.

No. No, someone at the airport might give the police a description of her as Nancy Clemons. She would have to leave town, but some way other than by plane.

She would dye her hair, buy some fake eyeglasses, and get another phony I. D. Then she would catch a bus to another state where she would make arrangements to fly to Switzerland. Her money was there. But it was in the name of Nancy Clemons. She couldn't walk into any traps.

Good thing I've got some of it strapped around my waist, she thought.

"Never put all your eggs in one basket," her father always said.

She would get some rest, and then she would put a new plan in motion. The house would be safe. The police had already done their investigation there. She still had her key. No, they had changed the locks. Well, she would just have to break a window. Simple.

Callie got back into the Colby house as planned with only a few small cuts on one of her legs to show for the effort. She was soaked. The storm had not let up a bit. She had tried to shield her head with a discarded newspaper she had found on the bus, but that had not been much shelter from the raging rain.

She went straight to Claire Colby's bedroom where she took a hot bath. Then she put together another wardrobe from the rejects in the closet. She threw the clothes in an old suitcase, took it downstairs and hid it under the bed in her old room.

Not much, but stylish and the best quality, she thought. It would have to do until she could replenish her wardrobe.

Callie contacted her man the next day, and he agreed to help her get another passport in another assumed name. This time, there would be no foul-ups—not on her part anyway.

But she had to find a way to get her money from her Swiss bank account. Maybe a few years down the line, she could go to that bank and claim the money as an inheritance from a long lost cousin, Nancy Clemons. Maybe over there, they wouldn't know about the robbery. Maybe they wouldn't even know about Nancy Clemons. But, wait, her bags had been checked through to Switzerland, so the police would certainly look for her there, especially with all that money in the bank.

Maybe she should head in another direction. Well, she would just take her time and figure this thing out. In the meantime, she would sell more of the Colby's paintings. She had sold a few of the small ones, and they had brought pretty big chunks of money.

Just think what the big ones would bring, she thought. If she could get them through the basement window, since that was the only way she could get in and out of the house now since that lawyer had deadbolts put on all the doors.

But, it must have been fate that brought her back here. For some reason, she had not gone down with that plane. She had been spared. And now she had a chance to replenish her money supply. Maybe she should just let the money in the Swiss account rot.

Callie had been hiding in the Colby house for three weeks before the broken basement window was discovered.

It certainly took them long enough to find out about it. Some house watcher that lawyer is, Callie thought. The night patrol officer had probably discovered it and called him.

Callie had heard Forrister's key in the front door. She had been in the kitchen about to fix herself some lunch. It was a good thing she hadn't started cooking. She hurried back to her room in the servants' quarters and crawled under the bed. A few moments later, she heard the basement door open. Forrister came back through the house a few minutes later cursing like he didn't have good sense. Then he left.

Callie was glad the window had been discovered. She had lain awake the first few nights wondering if some kook would discover it and come in the house on her. Now that it was going to be fixed, she could stop hiding in the servants' quarters and go on back upstairs to her fancy bedroom until she decided to leave.

She knew she should have been gone from the house, but she had not quite finalized her new plan. And she felt that the longer she stayed out of sight, the better her chances would be. She also felt comfortable there in the house where she had lived for so many years. It was home to her. As disturbed as its owners had been, it was a good house.

I had some of the best times of my life here, Callie thought.

A few hours later, the lawyer returned. "This way," Callie heard him say.

Then there were people all over the house. "Must be a dozen of them," Callie whispered to herself. *All those people to fix one window?* she thought

A few minutes later, Callie was hearing all kinds of noises: the buzz of drills, banging, chipping, and glass falling/breaking. The window in the basement being replaced?

"Does it take all that just to replace a window?" Callie asked herself. *And why so many people?* she thought.

Callie awoke a few hours later. She was shocked that the house was so quiet. "Oh, no. I must have fallen asleep," she said to herself. "Are they gone?" she whispered. She lay still, listening for several minutes then crawled out from under the bed. *It's already dark*, she thought.

She went out into the back hallway and over to the basement door. She stood for a moment with her ear to the door. *I don't hear a thing. They must be gone,* she thought. She quietly opened the door, stood another moment listening, then turned on the light and tiptoed down the steps into the basement.

The window had not only been replaced but now had bars on it. In fact, all the windows in the basement had bars

115

on them. Callie stood looking in awe at the ominous iron bars for a few moments. A thought hit her, and she raced back upstairs. She ran through the downstairs part of the house checking all of the windows. Bars. *The bedrooms upstairs*, she thought. She sprinted up the stairs to the second floor, racing from room to room only to discover that all the windows had bars on them.

"Bars all over the house," Callie said to herself. Her face was aghast. *And dead bolt locks on the doors*, she thought. Had to have a key for both sides.

"What am I going to do?" she whispered.

Callie was petrified.

"I'm locked in!" she screamed.

CHAPTER 12

Velma Hannah sat at her desk at The William E. Colby Agency. She smiled to herself as she thought about the meeting that had just ended—another meeting with Creative. This morning's meeting had been to commend the department for its excellent work during the past four months.

The company had begun to thrive again. Creative was at its best as was the head of that department.

Bradley Morris was good, and he knew it. He also knew that if he wanted to keep his good job, he had to shape up. He spoke courteously to his employer when he happened to see her (which was not too often lately). He stayed in his office now, producing, creating (like the boss lady had instructed him to do). His entire department was producing. Bradley saw to that.

How he detested the woman, and yet...Did he really?

Bradley did not know what to make of his feelings for Velma Hannah, the woman who was making his life a living hell. He wanted to hate her, and rightly so, but something inside him was not in agreement.

He made great efforts to stay out of his employer's way.

Velma could not have asked for a better arrangement.

Velma decided to keep William's assistant general manager in that position as acting assistant general manager until Sonya came on board. She had dreaded the unsavory task of officially demoting him to third in command. When she and Sonya inherited the two top positions, he was automatically pushed out of his post as second in command.

Tom Simms had been overwhelmed at first. His short, pudgy body had shaken, uncontrollably, when his new female—of all things—employer had given him the news. He even thought about quitting his job. But where would he find another at fifty-nine? Who would hire him? But the humiliation was just too much.

Then Velma had assured him he would still be the real assistant general manager while the girl learned the business—after assuming her position with the agency. She also guaranteed him that his salary would remain the same after his demotion to third in command. This last bit of news seemed to appease him. His workload would be lessened, but his salary would remain the same. Not a bad deal. Maybe he could tough it out after all.

The William E. Colby Agency was back on its feet— just like old times. It continued to thrive for the next four years.

CHAPTER 13

The young woman stepped off the plane. Her eggshell, light wool suit was expensive, and she wore it regally, her long legs gliding her slender frame through the crowded airport. Any woman would have given anything to own the jewelry that completed her ensemble. Her jet-black hair blew in the soft breeze. It had been freshly cut and styled prior to her leaving Paris the day before. Her oval shaped face was made up to perfection, but it appeared solemn and hard. Her blue eyes blazed, wildly, angrily—not focused. An air of mystique surrounded her.

The woman went swiftly through the terminal to the carousel area. She located the carousel on which her luggage would be arriving, signaled a porter, and they both stood— she, most impatiently—waiting. Presently, her luggage began coming down the chute.

The porter took the bags, many of them, out to one of the waiting taxicabs. The woman put a bill in the porter's hand. He helped her into the back seat of the cab and closed the door.

"Sixteen Twenty-Four Forest Lane East," the woman said to the cab driver and settled back in the seat for the ride home. The cab pulled away from the curb.

The woman smiled.

The cab pulled into the driveway. The driver got out of the car, went around to the other side, opened the back door and helped his passenger out of the car. While he gathered her luggage, the woman stood looking at the stately mansion she was about to enter, memories flooding her mind.

When the driver had all of the luggage out of the car, she led the way to the front door. The man was saying something about the weather as he trotted along behind her with several pieces of luggage. The woman wished this little man would stop trying to make conversation with her. She was in no mood to talk with anyone—not yet, and certainly not a cab driver.

She pulled a ring of keys from her handbag and unlocked the front door of the house. She led the way inside. When the driver finished setting her luggage in the foyer, she handed him a bill then closed and locked the door.

She had seen the bars on the front windows when they drove into the driveway. She wondered if they were really necessary—her lawyer's security measure. Why hadn't he just had a security system installed? Something she had been trying to get her mother to do for years, but her mother had been so trusting and had so much faith in her fellow humans. Well, she had trusted her husband, and look where that had gotten her.

Maurice was probably too lazy to come over in case someone tripped it, she thought. At least he had sense enough to change the locks and send her a set of keys.

She stood looking across the massive living room for a moment. Then she smiled, menacingly. A gleam appeared in her eyes. Her mind raced. Her thoughts excited her. She had waited for this moment a long time. Now she was ready to do what she had to do.

Sonya Ellis Colby was home.

Sonya walked into Maurice Forrister's office two hours later. She had changed into a plain, but elegant, two-piece suit. *More business like*, she thought. She was going to be a businesswoman now, and she had to look the part.

Maurice rose to greet her as she entered the office and was astonished at what he saw. The girl of a few years ago was no more. The strikingly beautiful young woman who stood before him, so poised and confident, was an altogether different person. Then she smiled—that snide, one-sided, malicious smirk that he had seen so many times. He knew that Sonya Colby was, indeed, back.

"Hello, Maurice," Sonya said.

"Hello, Sonya."

"Were you surprised to hear from me?"

"Yes, I was."

"Good. I love surprises."

"I know you do. Please sit down."

She did.

The lawyer sat behind his desk, laced his fingers and leaned back in his chair. "Tell me about Paris."

CHAPTER 14

"She has been gone for four years, for God's sake! After all this time... It's hard to believe she came back at all." Tom Simms was horrified. He paced in front of Velma's desk. His fat hands were jammed into his pants pockets. His little beady eyes darted angrily about the room.

"I know," Velma said. She stood behind her desk, a worried look on her face.

"Velma, I've been in this position for so long. I don't want to give it up. I wish—"

"Don't, Tom. It won't do any good. She's back."

"And back to stay, she says. She just marched in and moved me out of my office."

"Her office," Velma corrected him.

"Yeah, her office," Tom said shaking his head as if he could not believe what was happening. "She says you're next."

"No, Tom. That's where she's wrong." Velma's voice was calm but stern. "William Colby put me here, and I'm here to stay. I've worked hard these past four years rebuilding this agency. Lying awake nights, planning, scheming. I've surpassed even William's goals for this place. It's my life now. I won't let her take it away from me. I'm going in to see her."

"Good luck."

Velma left the office. Tom flopped languidly onto a chair in front of the desk. He bent over, holding his bald head in both hands. He was angrier than he had ever been in his life. He wanted to kill somebody.

"Welcome home, Miss Colby," Velma said. She closed the door to Sonya's office quietly behind her and braced herself for whatever was to come. She did not know what to expect from the girl. She did not dare even speculate.

The room looked like Tom Simms. Rather drab. Decorated in earth tone colors. Strictly masculine. Velma was sure the decorators would be in to redo the office to Sonya's specifications any day now.

Velma looked into the angry eyes of the young woman who sat behind the huge desk looking grossly out of place.

"Get out of my office, bitch!" Sonya hissed.

Velma strained to keep her voice calm. "No, Sonya—"

"Miss Colby to you," Sonya hissed.

"All right, Miss Colby, we need to talk. I know you don't like me."

"Wrong. I hate your guts. There is a difference." Sonya stood. Her eyes were piercing, wild.

"I'm sorry you feel that way. Nevertheless, we're running a business here. It would have been nice if you had at least called to let us know you were coming, so we could have prepared for you."

Sonya laughed. "Call? Before coming to my own company? I own this place."

"Half of it, Miss Colby. Just half of it. And you know what I mean. You've been away for over four years."

"This is my company, you conniving bitch, and I'll come and go as I please!" Sonya screamed.

"And I'm not going to be too many more bitches," Velma said as calmly as she could under the circumstances.

"What do you want me to call you? Stepmama? You didn't quite make it. At least my mother had sense enough not to give my father a divorce. That foiled your plans, didn't it?"

"Let's talk about now. Shall we? The business. Let's talk about how we're going to work together to keep this agency afloat."

"You shouldn't be here, you know. This should be all mine, but my lawyer tells me there's nothing I can do about that now."

"That's right, Miss Colby. Whether you like it or not, there has to be some kind of rapport between us if we're to run this agency smoothly."

Sonya looked scornfully at Velma for a moment then smirked. "Legally, that is. My lawyer says there's nothing I can do legally. You'd better watch your step, bitch."

She went past Velma out the door, slamming it behind her.

Velma stood for a few moments. She seemed at a loss as to what to do next. She finally went back to her office.

Tom Simms was gone. Where? He did not have an office anymore. *He'll be all right*, she thought. It wasn't as if he didn't know this was coming. She would have an office cleared for him.

Velma sat down at her desk and flicked the switch on the intercom.

"Yes, Miss Hannah?" Delia's voice came over the machine.

"Come in, please, Ms. Summers. I'd like to dictate a memo."

"Right away, Miss Hannah."

Velma dictated an interoffice memo to her secretary notifying all office personnel that Sonya Ellis Colby, Assistant General Manager, had assumed her position with the agency. Account executives were instructed to report to Sonya, via Tom Simms. Velma informed everyone that a meeting with the assistant general manager, Tom Simms, and department heads would be called as soon as the assistant general manager was settled in her office.

Sonya got into her red Ferrari that was parked on the Candry Square Office Building parking lot, and drove out onto Broadwalk Avenue. She turned the car south. She thought about her performance in the office a few minutes earlier. She had blown it. That was not the way she had planned to begin her first day at the agency—not if she wanted her plan to work. But when she went through the door, she could feel the rage building within her, and when she came face to face with the woman who had killed her mother—and her father—it had simply burst forth. She had been powerless to stop herself.

She would have to undo what she had just done in order to effectively initiate her plan. She had to gain the respect and trust of her enemy. She had to make others believe she could forgive and forget, that her only concern, now that she was older and wiser, was the progress of her late father's advertising agency.

Sonya decided that she had to practice self-control. She would rehearse herself in her new role—the role she had to play to perfection. For now.

An image of Velma Hannah flashed into Sonya's mind. Velma was on her hands and knees. Her body was broken, bruised, and bloody. Her mouth formed the word, "help." She repeated this gesture again and again, but no sound came from her lips. Sonya began to laugh. She laughed so hard she almost lost control of the car.

She pulled over to the side of the road and stopped. Suddenly, her laughter turned to sobs. She laid her head down on the steering wheel and cried, the tormented sounds coming from deep within her. Soon, she whimpered, and the sounds she emitted were likened to those of a wounded animal.

CHAPTER 15

The meeting with the assistant general manager and department heads was delayed for over a week, because Sonya did not return to the agency until the next Wednesday.

When Sonya walked in that morning, Velma, who was ready for battle, was pleasantly surprised. Sonya was all smiles and agreeableness—a completely changed woman.

Or was she? Velma did not know what to think.

The introductory meeting of department heads, Tom Simms, and the assistant general manager of The William E. Colby Agency went rather smoothly. Sonya told the assemblage that she was there for the benefit of the agency.

"I'm willing and prepared to do virtually anything to preserve the dignity of my father's dream." She looked at Velma, smiled, then shifted her eyes. "Oh, yes, there is one request I would like to make of all of you. I would like to be formally referred to as Sonya Ellis Colby. You are to address me as Miss Colby, of course, but all correspondence must bear my complete name. I'm sure most of you are aware that Ellis was my father's middle name also. You see, I'm afraid he wanted a boy when I was born. I disappointed him. If I had been a boy, perhaps matters would have turned out differently, especially here at The William E. Colby Agency."

Her eyes went back to Velma's face and held there as she paused, smiling sweetly. After a moment, she shifted her eyes, taking the others in at a glance. "I'm sure I shall enjoy working with all of you very much." Her eyes went back to and held on Velma.

Velma knew all too well that if Sonya had been a boy, she (Velma) probably would not have inherited half of The William E. Colby Agency.

All eyes followed Sonya's. Velma could feel them boring through her. Some of them, mocking her. She was upset, but she could not let Sonya see her discomfiture. They were waiting for her to say something, to retaliate perhaps. She glanced at Bradley Morris just in time to see a smile fade from his lips.

"Yes, perhaps circumstances would be different if you were a man, Miss Colby. But I'm sure your father still loved you very much. He also must have had faith in you. If not, he wouldn't have left you second in command at this company." Velma smiled then took them all in at a glance. "This meeting is adjourned." She looked at Sonya. "Unless you have something else to say, Miss Colby."

"No, I've said it all." Sonya smiled at Velma then added, "Except I'd like to say that I'm sorry about the other day. I'm afraid my conduct was inexcusable. Will you please accept my apology, Miss Hannah?"

"Apology accepted, Miss Colby." Velma's expression was one of surprise and skepticism.

Sonya stood and left the room. The others began to file out behind her.

Sonya went swiftly down the corridor to her office. Her mind raced. She would have to watch herself. She had done quite well at the beginning of the meeting, but she could take just so much of the woman at a time. Toward the end, she had gotten rather lax, until her public apology, of course. That had been a stroke of genius. She had apologized to the bitch right there in the meeting for everyone to hear—just in case word of her conduct of the week before had seeped to the employees. That should erase any doubts about her sincerity.

"Just control yourself, Sonya," she whispered to herself. "It won't be long now. You will have your revenge." She smiled, and then repeated. "You will have your revenge."

Velma was the last to leave the conference room. When she did, she went to her private bathroom and cried.

Sonya stopped at Cleavers, one of Baltonville's most popular upscale restaurants, for dinner after work that day. Then she went home. It was dusk. Her car lights and the lights outside the house were on, but she did not see the man who lurked behind a clump of shrubbery in the front yard.

He watched as Sonya pulled her car into the yard. He saw the automatic garage door go up, the car pull inside, and the door go down again.

The man's gaze shifted to the house. He watched as lights went on and then off downstairs. He knew that Sonya was, at that moment, going up the stairs to her bedroom. Visions of that room and past activities there flashed through his mind. The man moved out of the yard and walked across the street. He stopped at a point that allowed him a view of an upstairs window in the Colby house.

She was there all right, in her bedroom. The lights were on. *She's probably taking off her clothes about now*, he thought. He knew the routine well. She would go into the bathroom—naked. She would brush her teeth then sit at her vanity and remove her make-up. She would do a few more of the little things women, and especially beautiful woman, thought necessary before retiring.

The man stood at his post until he saw the lights go out in the upstairs room of the house across the street. He knew Sonya had finally gone to bed. He also knew that she wore either nothing or a thin, sexy nightgown (unless her taste in sleepwear had changed during the past four years). He hoped her dreams would not be pleasant ones.

Sonya was all smiles the next morning as she waltzed into Velma's office. "Good morning, Miss Hannah," she chirped.

Velma looked up, a stunned expression on her face. "Good morning, Miss Colby," she finally said, her voice apprehensive, her eyes glued to the younger woman's face, trying to get a clue as to what was really going on in her mind. "What can I do for you?"

"Oh, I just wanted to say good morning to you."

"Really." Velma was not convinced.

"Well, really, I wanted to say again that I'm sorry for the way I've been acting."

"Oh?" Velma looked at Sonya questioningly.

"Yes. I've been doing a lot of thinking during the past few days."

"The days you didn't show up for work." It was more a statement than a question.

"Yes. I guess I should have called, at least."

"At least. That would have been the thoughtful thing to do," Velma agreed. "Please, sit down."

"Thank you." Sonya sat on a chair in front of Velma's desk. "I am sorry," she said. "I needed that time to get my thoughts together, shall I say. I realize now that the chief concern to both of us is this agency and its continued success. I also realize that we must work together in order to accomplish that goal, and I'm willing to put my personal differences aside."

Velma smiled, uncertainly. "Needless to say, I'm happy you've reached that decision. I'm sure we can have an amicable working relationship."

"Oh, I want it to go beyond the office, Miss Hannah."

"Oh?" Velma looked at Sonya uncertainly.

"Yes. I'm sure we shall have dealings outside the company. Meetings with clients, et cetera. Father and Tom met regularly at the house to confer before meeting with the board. We shall probably need to do the same. And there's no reason why we can't have a sociable drink, or dinner, together occasionally, is there?" Sonya looked at Velma expectantly and smiled.

"No, I guess not."

"I don't blame you for being skeptical. I've really been acting like a spoiled child. I let my petty differences get in the way of duty. I'd like to erase all that. I want to think of myself as a responsible woman now. I want to do a good job here, and I want you to know that you can trust me."

"Well, Miss Colby, I don't know what to say. This is wonderful, but I have to tell you, it is a bit surprising."

"I'm sure it is, but I'd like to give it a try. How about you?" Sonya smiled sweetly at her prey.

"It's what I've been hoping for all along. It's what your father wanted."

"Then it's settled," Sonya said. "Oh, yes," she continued, "I'll need a temporary office. The decorators are coming in tomorrow morning to begin work in mine."

"Of course. I'll have one set up for you," Velma said.

"Thank you." Sonya rose and proffered her hand.

Velma took it.

Sonya left the office, the smile still pasted on her face. *Just a matter of time,* she thought.

Velma's eyes followed Sonya until the younger woman was out of the room. "What is your real agenda, Sonya?" Velma whispered, her question directed to the closed door.

And so it went for the next four weeks. Velma Hannah and Sonya Ellis Colby, the general and the assistant general managers, respectively, of The William E. Colby Agency were an item. They were together constantly: conversing, co-conducting meetings with the various departments of the agency, meeting with clients, lunching, and being quite friendly toward each other. They were even on a first name basis now. They got along like, maybe, mother and daughter?

These two former archenemies even talked about the forbidden subject, the man they had both loved. Sonya had brought up the subject of her father one evening over dinner. She said she had finally accepted the fact that he could have loved another woman, and that she would try not to hold that against Velma.

She had been most convincing.

Velma was beginning to think maybe William's dying request was not an impossibility after all. Maybe she and Sonya could be friends. She would certainly do her best to make that happen, because that was what William had wanted, and she had promised.

Sonya was proud of herself. She was actually pulling off this masquerade. What was the award great actors and actresses received? The Emmy? The Oscar? Whatever it was, if she were being nominated for this performance, she would certainly walk away with it. She was good. Sonya smiled to herself. She had the entire company fooled.

Not quite. There was one person who did not like the way things were shaping up between the general manager and her assistant. Bradley Morris had been observing Sonya when she thought no one was around. The woman was strange—extremely so. She seemed sincere enough, but not really. Something about her was just not right.

Bradley sensed that something was about to happen. He had no idea what, but he had a feeling it was not good. It was just a gut feeling that he could not shake. What was really baffling though was why he even cared.

CHAPTER 16

Sonya finally decided it was time to make her move. She walked into Velma's office one morning—all smiles. "Good morning, Velma," she chirped.

"Good morning, Sonya. How's your day going so far?"

"Well, average, I guess," Sonya said. She did not sound too enthusiastic.

"Oh? Is there a problem?" Velma asked.

"There is a favor I would like to ask of you."

"Yes?"

"I'd like to invite you to my house for cocktails Saturday night. A sort of tête-à-tête. I want to talk with you about my responsibilities here at the agency. You know the business so well, and I really want to do a good job."

"Of course, I'd be glad to help anyway I can, Sonya. We could meet right here in my office."

"I'd rather we didn't do it here, Velma. I want to look as professional as I can to our employees. Tom is a big help, but I seem to be catching on so slowly. Perhaps there are areas about which you are more competent than he. I wouldn't want him to know I had to come to you. It might be embarrassing to him if he found out."

Sonya concerned about someone else's feelings? Velma thought. A first, probably. "Tom is pretty thorough, Sonya. And remember, he was with the company long before I came on board."

"Please, Velma. I would appreciate it so much. Tom just doesn't seem to be getting through to me. But I think you would be of tremendous help. Maybe it's a woman thing." Sonya chuckled.

"Well, all right, Sonya, if it means that much to you."

"It does. Believe me. And, please, don't mention this to anyone. I'd be so embarrassed if my subordinates were to find out that I'm having such a hard time learning the business with both you and Tom training me."

"All right, Sonya. It will be our secret."

"Then I can expect you between seven, and seven thirty...?"

"Sounds good."

"Good. Thank you, Velma."

"You're welcome."

Sonya left Velma's office, all smiles. Velma turned her attention back to her work.

Sonya went through Velma's secretary's office, still smiling. She closed the door behind her, and her smile faded. She stood in the hallway for a moment, a combined look of rage, hate, and madness on her face. She moved hurriedly down the hallway to her newly decorated office. She went through the door, slammed it behind her, and went across the plush carpet to her shiny, new desk. She picked up a brass letter opener from a container on the desk, raised it above her head, and plunged it into the gleaming surface.

CHAPTER 17

Velma arrived at the Colby estate around seven-fifteen that Saturday night. Sonya welcomed her warmly. A few minutes later, they sat in the living room having cocktails. Velma was on the sofa; Sonya sat in a chair across from her.

"Thanks again for coming, Velma."

"No problem, Sonya. It was worth it. Your martinis are wonderful."

"They were the family's favorite drink. Father loved them."

"I know," Velma said. She felt awkward, in spite of Sonya's hospitality, sitting in William's house, discussing him with his daughter who had been her enemy only a few weeks earlier. They were on their second drink. They had talked, but every time Velma tried to bring the conversation around to the agency, and why she was there, Sonya had mentioned her father.

"Of course, you would know, wouldn't you?" Sonya was saying now, her voice sarcastic. "You knew everything about my father, didn't you, Velma?"

"No, Sonya, not everything. Look, I'm sorry if that was a difficult time for you. What can I say? We've been through this so many times. I thought you finally understood."

"You thought I finally understood? Did you really think I would ever accept my father taking up with the likes of you?"

"But, Sonya, I, I thought..." Velma's voice had begun to slur. Her eyes were getting heavy. She could hardly keep them open. "You said you..." she began again.

Sonya looked at her guest and smiled. Everything was going beautifully. "Is there something wrong, Velma?" she asked, her voice dripping with mock concern.

"Yes. Suddenly, I feel so tired. I can hardly keep my eyes open."

"Is that so? Let's talk about you and my father, shall we?"

"I'm supposed to be briefing you on, on..." Velma's head fell forward. She struggled to hold it up. "I, I," she stammered.

Sonya stood over Velma, her eyes blazing, her face distorted with rage. "Forget that! I want to know why you took my father away from us! My mother needed him! I needed him! I needed my father!"

"Sonya, I—"

"Shut up!" Sonya slapped Velma across the face. "Just shut up!"

Velma fell back onto the sofa. She tried to stand. Her head spun. Her legs buckled under her, and she fell back to the sofa again. "The drinks. You drugged me."

"That's right, bitch!" Sonya hissed. "You stole my father and drove my mother to suicide. Now I'm going to make you pay for that. For destroying my family! You're going to pay and pay good."

I've got to get out of here, Velma thought. "You're mad," she said.

"Shut up!" Sonya screamed and slapped her again. "You're going to pay for what you did! Do you hear me? You're going to pay!"

Velma tried to speak, but no sound came from her lips. She tried to get up but found that she could hardly move.

Sonya began to hit Velma about the head and face. She struck her again and again.

Velma struggled as best she could but was soon reticent. Sonya continued to strike her until she was too tired to raise her hand anymore.

She sank to the floor in front of the sofa, her breathing laborious. After resting a few moments, she got up, snatched Velma's purse from the sofa, and began searching through it. She pulled out a set of keys then left the room. She walked through the dining room and the kitchen into the mudroom where she opened the side door to the garage. She pressed a button on the wall beside the door, and the garage door went up. She went through it to Velma's car that was parked in the driveway. She got into the vehicle, fumbled with the keys until she found the right one, and started the engine.

A man stood behind the shrubbery in the front yard observing all this. In fact, he had been standing in the yard for over an hour now observing the activities about the magnificent house on Forest Lane East. "What the hell?" he whispered to himself as he watched Sonya drive Velma's car into the garage.

Sonya let the garage door down and went back through the house to the living room. She stood looking down on Velma who lay unconscious on the sofa.

"Bitch!" Sonya screamed. She struck Velma on the side of her face again. Then she grabbed her house guest by the arm and yanked her off the sofa to the floor. She put her arms through Velma's armpits and dragged her through the house to the basement door. She dropped her load, opened the door, then took her guest by the armpits again and begin pulling her down the basement steps. Velma's feet flopped on the stairs as they descended them, causing her to lose her shoes in the process.

Sonya pulled Velma to a far corner of the basement and let her body drop to the floor. She picked up some chains and manacles that lay nearby and fastened them to Velma's wrists and ankles. She started back up the stairs, stopped, picked up Velma's shoes, and threw them in the direction of the corner where she had deposited her

136

unconscious house guest. Then she continued up the stairs and on through the house into the living room where she gathered Velma's purse and scarf from the sofa. She carried the things down to the basement and threw them on the floor beside the still unconscious woman.

Sonya stood over her prey, clenching and unclenching her fists. She screamed, then whirled about, picked up a glass vase from a table nearby, and hurled it across the room. The vase shattered on the wall beyond. Sonya turned and raced back up the stairs.

Velma regained consciousness a few hours later. It was so dark. Where was she? She stood and was horrified to find that she could only move a few feet. Then she heard the clanking of the chains and realized her worst fears. Her shoes were gone, and the chains that bound her hands and ankles were anchored to the wall. From what she could make out in the darkness, her surroundings told her she was probably in a basement. Then she was still in the Colby house, Sonya's house, and she was being kept prisoner. Velma sat down on the floor, closed her eyes, and began to pray.

The man outside the Colby house decided that he had seen all he was going to see that night, so he moved from his perch behind the clump of shrubbery. He was puzzled about what he had witnessed. The notorious Velma Hannah arriving, and about an hour later, Sonya rushing out to pull her guest's car into the garage.

Now the house was dark. It was late, Velma Hannah had not left, and it appeared that Sonya had gone to bed.

Where was Velma Hannah? Was she a welcomed house guest for the night? Not likely. Not Velma Hannah. Not after all that had happened. If she were an overnight guest, she was certainly not a willing one. Another thought crossed the man's mind, and he knew that Sonya Colby was, indeed, capable of executing the horrible thing he had just envisioned.

The man walked off down the street to a parked limousine. He got in on the driver's side, took one last look at the Colby mansion, then closed the car door. He picked up a chauffeur's cap from the front seat, put it on his head, started the engine, and drove the car west on Forest Lane East.

Harry remembered the many times he had driven the Colby limousine down this street. He heard that the girl had her lawyer sell her mother's car when she left town. Harry missed that car. It was the best he had ever driven. He often wished for one just like it of his own.

Harry had tried to put his life back together after Sonya dismissed him from his position of chauffeur for the Colby family. It had been difficult. He had worked on three jobs during the past four years. The one he was on now was the only one that came close to paying what he had made while in the employ of the Colby family.

His lifestyle had changed drastically, and he did not like it one bit. He had tried to let bygones be bygones, to take the punches life threw him, but he found that bit of philosophy did not work for him. After a year of trying, he had turned his energies back to hating the woman who had taken from him the good life he had come to love and depend on so much.

Harry had done some checking and found out that Sonya had left the country. His source had also informed him when she returned to Baltonville. He had been watching her since that day.

He chuckled. "I think it's finally paying off," he said to himself. "I've got Miss Sonya Colby right were I want her. And now, it's my move."

Velma awoke suddenly. She sat up, startled. She could feel eyes on her. Then she saw someone standing over her, but she could not make out their features. It was a woman. But who was it? What was she doing? "Sonya?" she called softly.

The woman moved back a few steps and just stood looking at her.

Velma squinted up at the woman. Was it Sonya? No, it didn't look like Sonya. Who then? Why didn't she speak? "Hello. Who are you?" Velma said softly.

The woman moved away and disappeared up the stairs.

"What's going on here?" Velma whispered to herself.

In a moment, she heard a door open then close. If that had not been Sonya, then who? Was there someone else in the house?

She decided she would not allow herself to fall asleep again. It was too dangerous. She had to stay awake, keep her wits about her for whenever Sonya showed herself. She had to try to play on the younger woman's sense of decency.

Velma's chance came a few hours later. She knew it was day, because she could see traces of sunlight around the edges of the heavy curtains at the windows, and the room was a bit brighter.

She heard a door open, then the room was flooded with light. Yes, it did look like a basement. She heard footsteps. In a moment, Sonya was standing over her, smirking down on her. She held a tray with a covered dish and a glass of water in her hands.

"Good morning, Velma. Did you sleep well?"

I must be careful, Velma thought. "Sonya, you're troubled. Let me help you." Her voice was soft, almost pleading. "We can work this out if you will just give us a chance."

"I brought you some breakfast," Sonya continued as if Velma had not spoken. She set the tray on the floor beside Velma and made a grand gesture as she removed the cover. It held a single slice of bread.

"Enjoy!" Sonya said. Then she began to laugh.

Velma looked at the tray, astounded. "Sonya—" she began.

"You're my slave," Sonya interrupted, her voice quiet but venomous. "Did you know that, Velma? You're my slave. Look at your wrists. Your ankles. I've put you back in chains where you should have stayed. You'll wish you had before I'm through with you. You will wish you had never tried to live in my world. You will wish you had never laid eyes on my father. You will wish you had never been born." She paused for a moment then screamed, "You will wish you were dead!"

She took a moment to control herself then went on, her voice soft, calm again. "Since this is Sunday, I'm going to let you rest like the Lord says." Her voice became reverent, as she began to quote from the Bible. "'Remember the Sabbath day, to keep it holy.' The Bible said we shouldn't work on Sunday, Velma. Neither the master nor the servant, so that's why you will begin your work detail tomorrow morning."

"Work detail?"

"Oh, I have great plans for you. Believe me. There's a bathroom behind you. Your chains are long enough to allow you to use it. Have a nice day." She went up the stairs, turned out the lights, and closed the door.

Velma got up and looked about the room. Sonya said the bathroom was behind her. It was so dark, but her eyes were adjusting. She could just make out what looked like a door. She moved over to it. Yes, it was a door. She moved her hand over it until she felt the knob. She turned it, and the door opened. There was a light—a nightlight, plugged into a socket just above the face bowl. Velma flicked a switch beside the door. Nothing. She could see a light fixture overhead, but Sonya had probably removed the bulb. Well, the nightlight was something. Thank God for small favors. Then she noticed a washcloth and a bar of soap on the counter. "Thank you, Lord," she whispered.

Velma used the bathroom then washed up the best she could. She left the bathroom door open. At least the nightlight would provide a little light.

She ate the slice of bread and drank the glass of water. She then sat and watched the small stream of light at the window as it grew dimmer and dimmer. It was Sunday, and she was sitting on someone's basement floor eating bread and water. "Oh, God, help me," she implored.

Sonya brought Velma's dinner around six o'clock that evening. The light from the window was almost gone. Her dinner was a repeat of breakfast: a slice of bread and a glass of water.

"This will be your daily sustenance," Sonya said, smiling down on Velma.

"I can't live off this," Velma said.

"You'll live." Sonya turned, went back up the basement stairs, turned out the light, and slammed the door behind her.

The next morning, Sonya brought Velma's tray then hurried on into another room. Velma looked after her. She was petrified.

Sonya came back into the room dragging a bushel basket of peas behind her. On top of the basket sat a large stainless steel pan. "This is your job for today," Sonya said as if she were telling a child to wash the dishes. "I want every one shelled. If I find one pod unbroken when I return, you will be punished."

Velma could not believe her ears. She looked at the basket of peas then up at Sonya. "They smell, Sonya. What are you going to do with rotten peas?"

"I'm going to my office now at my company," Sonya continued as if Velma had not spoken. "It is mine, you know. My father didn't know what he was doing when he willed you half of our family's business. He was under a lot of stress. He was incompetent. He should never have given you what was rightfully mine, so I'm going to take it back, and this seems to be the only recourse I have. I believe I'm going to enjoy it thoroughly. Don't bother to scream while I'm gone. No one would ever hear you down here. You're my property now. My father bought you, and I inherited you. Now do as you're told, and you might live longer."

"Sonya, please. Think about what you're doing. What you're saying. You don't want something like this on your conscience. You—"

"Shut up!" Sonya lashed out, striking Velma across the face with the back of her hand. Then she whirled about and fled back up the stairs.

The lights went out, and Velma was engulfed in semidarkness again. She heard the door at the top of the stairs slam. She knew that she was, indeed, the prisoner of Sonya Colby. She also knew that the daughter of the man she had loved, her charge, was insane.

Sonya had driven out to the country to buy the peas—twenty bushels of them. The man had delivered them right away—during the first day of her week-long absence from the agency, the day she decided how she would proceed with her plan to dispose of Velma Hannah. The peas and the shackles had been simultaneous ideas. Brilliant. Her plan was working even better than she imagined.

CHAPTER 18

Sonya smiled sweetly and spoke pleasantly to her employees as she passed them on the way to her office that morning. After all, she did have something to smile about—at last. She stopped in her office briefly then went on down the hallway to Velma's office—a daily practice she had adopted, a morning ritual. "Good morning, Ms. Summers," she said, smiling sweetly.

Delia looked up from her work. "Good morning, Miss Colby."

"Is Miss Hannah in her office?"

"No, she isn't. I haven't heard from her today."

"Oh? She's usually here before I am. I suppose she has been detained. Please tell her I would like to see her when she arrives, will you?"

"Of course, Miss Colby." Delia resumed working.

Sonya left the office and went back down the hallway to her office smiling smugly to herself.

Word seeped through the William E. Colby Agency that Velma Hannah had not come to work or reported to anyone at the company that day. There were many speculations as to her whereabouts. By the middle of the day, most of the employees had begun to worry about their employer.

Bradley Morris was among them. In spite of their differences, he had to admire the woman.

When Bradley heard the news about Velma's absence from the company, his first impulse was to panic. Then he tried to dismiss all negative thoughts from his mind. She probably just decided to take a few days off, he told himself. She would probably call before the day was over. Or, perhaps, she was called out of town during the weekend and had not been able to get a message to the company yet.

Velma Hannah had it all together. She was one of the most together people he had ever known. *Then why hasn't she at least called?* he thought. He finally settled down enough to go to work, but thoughts of his boss still raced through his mind.

Tom Simms was another employee who was concerned about his employer. His employer. He preferred not to think of the woman in that capacity, but, unfortunately, he had no choice. He certainly did not think a woman, and especially a Black woman, should have been given such a lavish gift as a multimillion dollar firm—if only half. But Velma Hannah had been fair with him. He had to admit that. Perhaps that was why he stood in Sonya's office later that afternoon.

Or, perhaps, there was another reason.

"Yes, Mr. Simms, what can I do for you?" Sonya asked.

"Well, since we didn't hear anything from Miss Hannah today, I thought since you're new to the agency, maybe I could help out in her office until she returns. Uh, if she hasn't returned by tomorrow, that is."

"Yes, you have been a tremendous help to me today, Mr. Simms. If, in fact, we don't hear from Miss Hannah by tomorrow morning, perhaps you should work from her office." Sonya smiled up at him. "That would save us having to route matters, that are usually handled there, to another office. Do you think you could manage in that capacity, Mr. Simms?"

"Of course, Miss Colby." He was, of course, insulted.

"Well, we certainly hope she won't be gone long. Don't we, Mr. Simms?"

"Yes, Miss Colby. Of course."

"Yes," Sonya said, and her mind veered for a moment. A faraway look crept into her eyes.

Tom stood fidgeting uncertainly.

"Is there something else, Mr. Simms?" Sonya asked.

"This is so unlike her, Miss Colby. She hasn't missed a day in the last four years."

"Yes, I hear she opens and closes the place." She indicated a chair in front of her desk. "Sit down, Mr. Simms. Perhaps we should discuss this further just in case Miss Hannah has decided to take some time off."

"Thank you." He sat.

Sonya Colby and Tom Simms looked at each other. She saw the greed in his eyes. He saw, but did not want to believe, the madness in hers.

Tom Simms flopped his rotund frame into the chair behind the desk in his third-in-command office after his talk with Sonya. He still sat there, over an hour later, repeatedly running his hand over the bald spot on top of his head, his eyes flitting about the room. He was thinking about his present situation with The William E. Colby Agency. For over four years, he had been thinking about it, and now that it had come to a head, he seemed powerless to do anything about it.

Tom was certainly not satisfied with his present position at the agency. He wanted more. He deserved more. He wasn't a male chauvinist, but he really did not think a man of his caliber should have to answer to anyone, and certainly not to a woman—two women in this case. A young White woman who did not have a clue about what she was doing—and who did not even care—and an over-zealous Black one. A company of this magnitude needed a man at the helm, and he was that man. Why couldn't William Colby have seen that? What could the man have been thinking?

"He wasn't thinking," Tom said out loud. *He was just feeling*, he thought. *He let his emotions get in the way of reasoning.*

What had that woman done to him to make him do such an asinine thing as give away his company? There should be laws against such inheritances.

Tom had tried to understand, to be reasonable about the situation, but he could not fight his true feelings anymore.

He should have been made general manager. He was next in line. He had spent the best years of his life helping to build this agency. He had given his all. He knew the business probably as well as William Colby himself. He might have been able to work with Velma Hannah as his assistant, but this... If Colby wanted to do something for the woman, he should have made her his (Tom's) assistant. That would have been the right thing to do. The best thing for the company.

Men were rapidly losing their places in the business world to overbearing, clamoring, and unscrupulous female opportunists like Velma Hannah. These women were pushing men out of their rightful places on the job, in society, even in the home—either by some political or devious female maneuver or some bizarre twist of fate. Men should guard against such things. They should stand up for their rights while they still had the upper hand.

If they weren't careful, they were going to wake up one morning and find some woman sitting up there in the White House calling herself the president. Then it would all be over. They should incorporate laws that would legally keep women in their rightful places. He was certainly for such a move.

If only he had a voice in such matters.

As for Sonya, Colby's crazy daughter, trying to train her to do his job was a total waste of his time. Why should he anyway? Maybe he had a good discrimination suit. Maybe he should sue. Call F. Lee Bailey. No, he guessed he should not call him. He'd probably have to be accused of murdering somebody first.

"Don't tempt yourself," he whispered.

Somewhere in the recesses of his mind, Tom Simms hoped Velma Hannah had met with some unfortunate fate during the weekend that would prevent her from ever returning to the agency. Second-in-command was better than third any day even if he would be under the command of a lunatic. That girl was stark raving mad.

Velma sat on the floor in the Colby's basement surveying her situation. It was a dire one, but she would try not to let it break her spirit. Surely someone would find her. The police. Someone from the agency.

She was hungry, tired, angry, and scared. She told herself she would not eat the bread and drink the water Sonya left for her, but she had been so hungry around the middle of the day, she had gobbled down the bit of food and drink.

One thing she did not do though was shell the peas. She would not be put into servitude. She would not be anyone's slave. Those days were over for her people.

CHAPTER 19

Sonya stayed late at the office that evening. After all, she had to make things look good. She was in command now. She was running her company, as she should have been in the first place. She had to prove to everyone that she could, in fact, take her late father's place as the head of The William E. Colby Agency.

So, the great Miss Hannah had opened and closed the place.

Whatever it takes, Sonya thought.

She stopped at one of her favorite restaurants for dinner then went home. She was eager to see how her captive had fared. She had finally gotten her hands on the bitch. All the years of planning and scheming had paid off. She was going to make the woman pay, and pay she would, for what she had done to her family.

Sonya pulled her car into the driveway and pressed the garage door opener. The door went up. The light in the garage came on simultaneously with the opening of the door. Sonya pulled her Ferrari into the garage and parked it next to Velma's Jaguar.

Harry Reynolds moved swiftly from behind the shrubbery next to the garage where he had been crouching for sometime now and slipped in through the opening. The door came down, and Harry moved around to the driver's side of Sonya's car.

Just as Sonya opened the door to step out of the car, she saw Harry's reflection in the side mirror. She tried to slam the door shut, but it was too late. Harry grabbed it and yanked it open.

"Hey, baby. How're you doing?" he said. He offered her his hand.

"What do you want, Harry?" she snapped.

"I just wanted to see you. I told you we'd meet again. Remember?"

Sonya stepped out of the car, ignoring his outstretched hand. "Get off my property, Harry," she snapped. "If you're not off my property in two minutes, I'm calling the police."

"Now is that anyway to talk to an old friend? In fact, I remember when we were much more than friends." Harry touched her cheek. "Remember, baby?"

Sonya slapped his hand away. "Keep your hands off me!"

"All right. But there was a time when I didn't have enough hands for you. I guess your memory is a bit shorter than mine. I remember those nights just like they were yesterday. We could pick up right where we left off. I'm as much man as I ever was, and you're definitely a lot more woman. Did those boys in Paris make you feel as good as I did?"

He tried to kiss her, and she slapped him.

"Get out of my face," she hissed. "I'm warning you! Get off my property! Now! Or, I swear I'll call the police."

He grabbed her wrist. "I don't think you want to do that."

"Let go of me!" She jerked free of his grasp.

"I really don't think you want to call the police," Harry said, rubbing his jaw where she had slapped him. He walked over to Velma's car and touched the hood. "Whose car is this? Do you have a house guest?"

"That's none of your business."

Harry walked back over to Sonya. "I'm making it my business. I know whose car it is, and I know what you've done to her."

Sonya looked at him for a moment, and then laughed. "I don't know what you're talking about."

"Oh, yes, you know, all right. But it can be our secret. Yours and mine."

"What do you want, Harry?"

"Money. What else?"

"And you think I'm just going to give you money?"

"I think so." He indicated the door. "Let's go inside and talk it over, shall we?"

"I don't want you in my house, Harry."

"I'm going to talk to somebody about what I know."

Sonya hesitated a moment then unlocked the door, and they went into the house. Harry closed the door. They went on through the house to the living room.

"May I sit down?" he asked.

"Suit yourself," she snapped.

He sat on the sofa, leaned back and crossed his legs. He looked...most comfortable.

"Now, what's on your little mind, Harry?"

"Miss Velma Hannah is on my mind right now and how much it means to you to keep my mouth shut about what I know."

"And just what do you know?"

"I know Velma Hannah came here Saturday night. I also know she never left. I know her car is in your garage. Shall I continue?"

Sonya looked at him with rage in her eyes. "I have no fight with you, Harry."

"What do you plan to do with the car? Surely you're not going to leave it here. Perhaps I could help."

"I don't need your help, Harry. I don't want your help."

"Fine. When her disappearance is discovered, I'll offer my assistance to the police."

"So now you're stooping to blackmail?"

"Whatever it takes."

"How much?" Sonya asked after a brief moment of hesitation.

"Two hundred thousand."

Sonya laughed. "You're crazy."

"For murder? I think that's a fair price."

"Murder? I haven't murdered anyone, Harry. You don't know as much as you think you do."

"Then what have you done with her?"

Sonya looked at him, her eyes flashing. "Stay out of my business."

"Look, you'd better deal with me if you know what's good for you."

"You've always been a greedy bastard, Harry. One day, you're going to regret your avaricious nature. Be careful it doesn't get you killed."

"Forget the empty threats, Sonya. Do we deal? Or do I go where my information will be appreciated?"

"I will not give you two hundred thousand dollars."

"Then we don't deal."

"That's too much. I'll give you one."

"No deal. You've got a lot of work to do, and you'd better do it within the next few minutes, because I've changed my mind. When I leave here, I'm going straight to the police. I hope you know what you plan to do with the body and your victim's car."

"I haven't killed her, I told you."

"Then where is she?"

"Forget it, Harry."

"Look. I swear. This will be it. I won't come back for more if that's what you're thinking. You'll be home free," Harry said.

"I could kill you."

Harry stood and reached into his coat pocket. "Don't try it." He pulled out a gun and pointed it at Sonya. "You make a move I don't like, and you'll join Velma Hannah wherever she is. I know you've done something to the woman, so there's no need trying to deny it. Now, do we have a deal?"

Sonya stood for a moment, her mind racing, scheming. "All right, Harry," she finally said. "Maybe I can use your help after all."

"That's better," Harry said. A coy smile played on his lips.

"We'll see." She turned and started toward the back of the house. "Come with me, and put that gun away."

"No way, baby. I don't trust you."

Sonya stopped, turned back to Harry and smirked at him. "Then how are we going to do business, Harry? I'm just a woman. Are you afraid of a little woman? A big strong man like you?"

"No, I'm not afraid of you."

"Then put the gun away. I don't want you to frighten my guest." She turned and walked away.

Harry chuckled and put the gun back inside his coat pocket. No, he wouldn't need it anymore. She had been sufficiently scared into doing what he wanted. Yes, Sonya Colby was ruthless, but she had now met her match.

Harry was proud of himself. He was already formulating in his mind how he was going to spend his two hundred thousand dollars.

Harry followed Sonya through the dining room, the kitchen, then into the back hallway to the basement door.

Velma heard the door at the top of the stairs open. The lights went on, and she heard footsteps on the stairs. She had heard Sonya come in earlier. So she was finally coming down to see about her. No, it sounded like more than one person. Could it be someone else? The police?

Sonya and Harry came into view, and Velma's hopes soared. Sonya's eyes went straight to the basket of peas. She let out a piercing scream then picked up some of the peas and hurled them at Velma. Her eyes were wild, her lips curled back in a snarl.

"How dare you defy me! I'm your mistress, slave! You will do as I command!" Sonya slapped Velma then picked up the basket of peas and dumped them on Velma's head.

Harry looked on in horror. He could not believe his eyes. Did Sonya actually have the woman in chains? He knelt beside Velma and checked the manacles that bound her wrists.

"Help me. Please help me," Velma pleaded.

Sonya saw her chance. She picked up the empty pan and raised it above her head. Velma screamed. Sonya hit Harry on the side of the head with the rim of the pan. Harry slumped to the floor, his eyes closed. Sonya took the gun from his coat pocket, and began beating him about the head with it.

"Stop, Sonya!" Velma screamed. "You'll kill him! You'll kill him!"

Sonya stopped, between blows, the gun suspended in midair.

Blood oozed from several cuts on Harry's head and face. Sonya laid the gun down on the floor, making sure it was out of Velma's reach. Then she put her arms through Harry's armpits and dragged him into another room. She reappeared, picked up some rope that lay in a corner and went back into the other room.

Sonya struggled to pull Harry up into a large leather chair. After a few minutes, she had accomplished her task. She tied his upper arms and shoulders to the top of the chair, ran the rope down to his hands, and tied them in front of him. Then she ran the rope down to his feet, tied them together, then ran the ends around the back of the chair and tied them together.

Satisfied that her victim was completely at her mercy, Sonya raced back into the outer room where Velma sat with her head in her hands. Sonya stood over Velma, sneering down on her, her face distorted with rage.

"You're going to learn when I tell you to do something, I mean for you to do it! Do you hear me?"

She hurried off into another room. In a few moments, she rushed back in the room with a whip dangling over her right shoulder. She began to lash at Velma with the whip—wildly—striking her wherever the whip happened to land. Velma turned on her side and balled herself up into a knot, covering her face and head, trying to protect herself as best she could. The whip came down on her back, arms, and legs again and again—until Sonya was too exhausted to raise it anymore.

Sonya sank to the floor, breathing heavily. After a few moments, she rose and looked down on Velma who still lay curled up, holding her head, low whimpering sounds coming from deep within her.

"For your impertinence, you will not be given dinner tonight," Sonya said calmly. "Tomorrow, your workload will be doubled. Good night." She snatched up the tray she had brought down that morning, then the gun from the floor, and started for the stairs.

Whatever she did to the scheming wench was too good. There was no way she could gain complete satisfaction for what the woman had done to her family, but she was certainly going to try. Maybe she should have killed her. Her and that fool in the other room.

The lights went out, and Velma heard the door at the top of the stairs slam. She could not believe what was happening to her. The girl had actually whipped her like a slave. She was, indeed, in the clutches of a mad woman. She and the man. Who was he? And how had he gotten himself involved in this? Velma wondered if he was still alive.

Sonya marched through the mudroom, out the door and on into the garage. She flicked on the light and then picked up an axe that sat up against the far wall.

She remembered the day her father had brought it and a hatchet home—many years ago. The axe was for him, the hatchet for her. The two of them had gone out into the woods to cut down a Christmas tree. They had brought it back to the house and she, her father, and mother had decorated it. Decorating the Christmas tree had been a family ritual for many years. Those were some of her favorite times with her father.

Until things had gone wrong. Until Velma Hannah. Sonya missed those close moments with her father. She missed…her father.

Her father had provided her with one last use for this celebrated axe. She raised it above her head and went toward the metallic gold Jaguar. She smashed the axe through the Jaguar's windshield then moved slowly around the car, bringing the axe down on the gleaming surface again, and again, and again.

Velma's entire body hurt. Blood oozed from her back, arms and legs where the whip had cut through her clothes into her skin. She continued to pull her clothing away from her body to keep them from sticking to her.

The man in the next room had come to. Velma had been listening to him call for Sonya for what seemed like hours. *At least he's alive*, she thought. But he was hurt badly. He sounded so weak. He knew Sonya. Was he one of her friends? Maybe he was a friend but not anymore. He was now a prisoner just as she, both of them at the mercy of Sonya Ellis Colby.

Velma was too distressed to try to sleep. She sat listening to the man calling to Sonya, his voice getting weaker and weaker. Eventually, he grew silent, and Velma knew that either the worst had happened, or he had finally given up his attempts to summon Sonya.

The door at the top of the stairs opened, and Velma heard cautious footsteps descending. In a few moments, she could make out the form of a woman standing over her. She held a wash pan in her hands. The woman set the pan on the floor then walked over and turned on a small lamp on a table that sat on the wall beyond. She walked back over to Velma, knelt beside her and pulled the bloody blouse up over her head. She began to wash Velma's wounds.

"Who are you?" Velma whispered.

The woman did not answer but continued her task. She finished washing Velma's wounds then began rubbing some kind of ointment on her body. It was cool and soothing.

"Thank you," Velma whispered. When the woman did not answer her, she continued, "There is a man in the next room. He's hurt, too."

The woman still did not speak.

"Will you help him? He's tied with a rope. You can untie him, then he can help me," Velma tried again, desperation setting in about now.

The woman continued what she was doing, saying nothing. Velma decided it was useless trying to talk to this person who was trying to help her. She had not responded to a thing Velma had said.

"Thank you. I feel much better," Velma said.

The woman finished with the ointment, helped Velma straighten her clothes, and then gathered her things. She turned out the lamp and started back up the stairs.

"No, come back. Please. Who are you?" Velma whispered, her voice desperate. "Please, don't go. Come back."

The woman went on up the stairs.

In a few moments, Velma heard the door at the top of the stairs open then close. "Please, God, let her help us," she implored. Did she dare hope?

Velma was hungry. She wished for the slice of bread and the glass of water that had been denied her. "Dinner," she said to herself, her voice bitter. *A slice of bread and a glass of water, and I couldn't even have that, because I was impertinent to my mistress*, she thought.

Velma thought of the irony of her situation, and chuckled in spite of herself.

Later, she shelled some of the peas that lay about her on the floor and ate them.

CHAPTER 20

Whatever the mysterious woman had put on Velma's wounds had literally stopped the pain. Velma was eternally grateful. She just wished she knew the identity of the person to whom she owed her gratitude.

She was beginning to nod off when the first stomach pains hit her. Immediately she thought of the peas. They were spoiled, and she shouldn't have eaten them. But she had been so hungry. She spent the next few hours in and out of the bathroom, with diarrhea, vomiting her insides out, and in excruciating pain.

Her stomach was just beginning to settle when traces of sunlight began to show around the edges of the curtains at the basement windows.

A short time later, she heard the door at the top of the stairs open and Sonya's footsteps descending. Velma braced herself. She knew she was dealing with a maniac and that she was in no position to protect herself. At first, she thought she could use her mind, her intellect, to try to reason with the younger woman. Now she wasn't so sure. Sonya seemed beyond reasoning. But what else could she do? She couldn't just lie down and die. She had to fight.

Sonya walked over to Velma and stood glaring down on her for a few moments. She wore a housecoat and slippers and carried a tray in each hand. They each bore a single slice of bread and a glass of water. Sonya set Velma's tray on the floor beside her.

"Good morning," she said. Her voice was surprise-ingly calm.

"Sonya, you must get a doctor. That man. You hurt him badly. He could die."

"You're both going to die sooner or later. So, you see, it really doesn't matter, now does it?" She went on into the room, where her second captive awaited his fate, with the other tray. "Good morning, Harry. Did you sleep well?"

Harry looked up at Sonya. She smiled and seemed to take delight at seeing the results of her handiwork. Harry's right eye was swollen half shut, his face was covered with dried blood, and his clothes were stained where blood had dripped on them from the wounds on his head and face.

"My, my, your appearance is terrible. You don't look a thing like your old, sexy self, lover man. It was a pleasure having you come visit me last night. Didn't we have fun?" Sonya continued. She laughed.

"What do you do for kicks now, Sonya? Torture people?" Harry said.

"Only when they get in my way, you clumsy bastard. My fight was not with you. You forced your way into this. Now deal with it."

She set the tray on his lap, and he dumped it onto the floor.

Sonya laughed. "Oh, I'm so sorry, sir. I should have known you would want to clean up before dining. I'll bring you some water and a washcloth." She chuckled again. Then her smile faded, and she said sternly, "But I won't bring you anymore food until this evening, and it will consist of the same thing: one slice of bread and a glass of water. I suggest you think about that during the day." She turned and started out of the room.

"Sonya!" Harry shouted.

Sonya turned back to him. "Yes, Harry?"

"Look, I, I'm sorry," he stammered. "Let me go, and I'll never bother you again. I promise. I'll leave town right away. Or I'll do anything you want. I'll even help you with her. I don't want any money. Not a cent. She shouldn't have done what she did. She deserves anything you do to her."

"Shut up, Harry. You barged your way into this. Now you're in it to the finish. Congratulations." She left the room, closed the door behind her, and walked over to Velma.

"You know the police are going to be looking for us, Sonya. For me and the man," Velma said.

"Let them look," Sonya said. "They'll never suspect me." She went into the room where she kept the peas and pulled out another basket. She dragged it over to Velma. "These and all the others around you had better be shelled when I get home this evening, or else."

The two women looked at each other, and Sonya could see the fear in her victim's eyes. Oh, she was trying hard to mask it, but it was there. Sonya did not want to have to beat her again with the whip. Some of the cuts might become infected and set up blood poisoning. She might die, and Sonya did not want that. Not yet. She wanted her to suffer the way she and her mother had suffered when the woman took her father away from them. She wanted her to die slowly—a little bit every day for the next year or two.

"They'll come, Sonya. But if you let me go now, I won't press charges. I'll say it was all a mistake."

"I don't need any favors from you!" Sonya screamed.

Velma swallowed hard and decided to press Sonya further. "You have everything going for you, Sonya. Why do you want to mess up your life with a kidnapping? No, you'll be charged with two kidnappings now, and possibly attempted murder."

"You messed up my life when you took my father away from me. So you just shut up! Just shut your mouth!" Sonya turned and ran up the stairs.

"Sonya! Sonya, listen to me!" Velma called after the fleeing woman.

The door at the top of the stairs slammed.

***

Sonya returned a few minutes later with some writing paper, an envelope, and a pen. She threw the items on Velma's lap. "Write!" she commanded.

"What?" Velma looked at Sonya in total bewilderment then down at the writing paraphernalia. *A suicide note?* Velma thought. *If I do that, she will kill me for sure.* "What do you want me to write?"

Sonya began to pace up and down the floor like a caged animal, her mind racing, confused. She finally turned to Velma.

"You're going to write me a letter. To the company."

"What? Sonya—" Velma began.

"Shut up! Let me think." Sonya paced some more, in deep thought. "You will tell me," she finally said, "that you have decided to go away for a while. That you have come to terms with the reality of what you did to the Colby family. You will say that your sin is so overwhelming you can't live with it any longer. Somehow, you have to make amends. Therefore, you are relinquishing your half of the William E. Colby Agency to its rightful owner, Sonya Ellis Colby, daughter of the late William Ellis Colby, and proper heir."

"No, Sonya, I will never give up my share of the agency."

Sonya leered at Velma, astounded for a moment, and then she raced into the room where she kept the whip. In a moment, she was back, the whip raised above her head, ready to strike. "Don't you tell me what you won't do! Do you understand me? I give the orders, and you follow them!"

Velma flinched. She closed her eyes for a moment. In her mind, she could feel the whip tearing into her flesh. If, by some miracle, she were to survive this ordeal, her body would be scarred for life.

"Now write!" Sonya ordered.

"My cat," Velma said, her voice hopeful. "I would never go away and leave my cat unattended. The police would know something had happened to me."

Sonya paced for a moment, thinking. Velma looked uneasily at her.

"What's your cat's name?" Sonya finally asked.

"Geronimo," Velma said.

Sonya turned to Velma, a smirk on her face. "Would you like to have Geronimo here with you, Velma?"

Oh, no, Velma thought. *She's going to get him. I should never have mentioned him. I should have—*

"Answer me!" Sonya's voice thundered through Velma's thoughts.

"Yes," Velma whispered.

"Speak up!"

"Yes." Velma's voice was a bit louder this time. Her mind raced. She berated herself for having mentioned the cat. "But you won't be able to get into my building. It's secured, and we have a watchman on duty around the clock."

"Let me worry about that." Sonya chuckled. "Write the letter and have it ready in ten minutes. I'm going in early this morning. Since the other half of The William E. Colby Agency management team has deserted the company, all the workload has fallen on my shoulders, so to speak. I'm having to work extra hours to keep things afloat—with Tom Simms' help, of course. Oh, by the way, I told Tom he could use your office until you return. I do believe he's enjoying himself tremendously. That's one person I don't think will miss you at all, Miss Hannah. In fact, he's probably praying that whatever has happened to you will be permanent.

"Now I've told you what I want you to say in the letter. Compose it in your own words. You're a secretary. Make it sound good. You should have stayed downstairs in the secretarial pool, Velma. The day you became my father's assistant was the day you sealed your fate." She turned and went back up the stairs.

Velma began to write. Her mind raced. Sonya was planning to kill her. She had to think of some way to save herself from the clutches of this insane woman. She had to let somebody know what was happening to her.

She could not think of any kind of clue to put in the letter.

In a few minutes, Sonya reappeared with a small pan of water, some soap, and a hand towel. She went into Harry's room. "Here you are, Mr. Reynolds." She threw the soap and the towel into the pan, then set the pan on his lap.

"I *need* a doctor," Harry said, as he wrung out the towel and wiped gingerly at his face.

"What for, Harry? No doctor in the world could help you now. You're completely in my care. Let's just say I'm your doctor. Hurry up. I have to go to work." She left the room and went back over to Velma. "Have you finished the letter?"

"Yes." Velma handed the letter and an addressed envelope to Sonya.

Sonya read the letter, slowly, as if dissecting every word, then smiled. "Very good. I couldn't have done a better job myself. Thank you." She laid the letter on the table that held the lamp then went back into Harry's room. "Have you finished grooming your handsome self, Mr. Reynolds? Well, you do look a little better, but just a bit. Tut, tut. You really should take better care of yourself."

She picked up the pan from his lap. "Have a nice day." She left the room, closing the door behind her. She went on into the bathroom. A moment later, she came out of the bathroom and walked back over to Velma. "I'll bring you a nice surprise this evening." She picked up the letter from the table and went on up the stairs.

In a few moments, Velma heard the door to the basement close and the lock slide into place.

CHAPTER 21

Sonya deposited the letter in a mailbox on the way to work. Velma had done just as she had been instructed. The letter was perfect. No one could question its validity. Sonya had found stamps in her mother's bedroom. That had been one of her mother's pet things. She always kept stamps of all denominations on hand. She had been so thorough, always kept everything at the ready.

It was the first time Sonya had been in her mother's room since she had come back home. It looked...lived in. No dust. It was as if everything had been covered. But it hadn't. She had not thought to cover the furniture before she left for Paris, and Maurice certainly would not have done so without her having to tell him. The bathroom sparkled. It, especially, looked as if it were being used daily.

But she knew that was impossible.

Another enigma about the house was a huge pile of compacted trash bags she had found in one of the rooms in the basement a few days after she returned home. She had called Waste Management and had them removed; but why had they been there? She was sure the trash from the house had been picked up weekly, or someone had not been doing her job. Matilda? Callie? But why? Why take trash down to the basement rather than out to the curb for pickup?

Maurice had told her about the robbery. She should have called him sooner. At least he had saved some of her mother's jewels. The thieves had left the most expensive pieces behind. Strange. Probably kids who did not know the value of such priceless gems.

Sonya had put those jewels back in the safe in her mother's bedroom that morning. Not that anyone could break into the house now with bars everywhere, but she felt better with them locked in the safe.

Sonya did not like the feeling she had when she was in her mother's room. She had not been in there since she had the carpet replaced before leaving town four years earlier. She would stay out of that room unless it was absolutely necessary for her to go in there—as it had been that morning.

She might have been recognized purchasing stamps at the post office—if the police were smart enough to put two and two together about the mysterious letter. So going into her mother's room had been a necessary evil, so to speak.

She couldn't imagine what would prompt her to enter that room again though. It looked as if her mother were still occupying it.

She thought of her mother—lying there on the floor of that room with her throat cut by her own hands. Then she thought of her mother's real murderer—and revenge.

The letter should arrive at the office tomorrow morning, she thought.

"You can rest now, Mother. I'm going to make everything all right," she said out loud.

Sonya had dressed carefully that morning. She looked resplendent in a Paris original, raw silk, mint green suit. At the last minute, she chose a favorite jade brooch—a gift from a past admirer—that completed her attire to perfection. This was a time for celebration, and that brooch always put her in a festive mood.

Sonya thought about Harry and how the ignorant man had almost foiled her plan. Trying to blackmail her? Surely he had forgotten who she was.

Had he honestly thought she would give him two hundred thousand dollars to keep his mouth closed? Sonya began to laugh. "Not on your life, Harry. Not when there are other ways to shut your mouth," she said out loud between gales of laughter.

Velma was the subject of most conversations around The William E. Colby Agency. There was concern: genuine, and of a sense of duty, of course. After all, she was their employer.

Sonya played her role well. She managed to look as worried and concerned as any of the others. She talked with security and told them if no word was heard from Miss Hannah by the end of that day (the second day of her absence) she wanted them to go to her house the next morning to check on her. If their investigation there proved fruitless, she would then take the initiative of calling the police. But she wanted everyone to know that she was concerned about prying into Velma's private life.

Some of the employees were beginning to like Sonya, especially the ones who did not think too much of Velma Hannah's inheritance into the company. Others were skeptical of the assistant general manager.

Bradley Morris was among the latter. He stood outside Sonya's office door now. He took a moment to prepare himself to go inside and speak with the shifty-eyed, mysterious woman. In spite of her efforts to appear to be caring and amicable toward Velma, Bradley knew there was a sinister side to her.

He was determined to follow through on his hunch that things were not well with Velma Hannah and that Sonya Colby might be responsible.

Bradley opened the door and went inside. "I'm here to see Miss Colby," he said to Lisa Odom, Sonya's secretary.

"Oh, yes, Mr. Morris, she's expecting you," Lisa said. "Please go right in."

Bradley did so.

"I'll be with you in a moment, Mr. Morris," Sonya said as he entered the room. She was busy with some paperwork on her desk. "Please have a seat."

"Thank you," Bradley said. He closed the door behind him, walked over, and sat on a chair in front of Sonya's desk.

And what a desk it was. He had heard about the newly decorated office of the assistant general manager, but this was his first time seeing it. No wonder the renovations had taken so long. Everything had been imported, he was told: the designer wallpaper, the carpet, the furniture—even the toilet seat, someone had said.

I'd like to see that, he thought. Maybe he should go take a leak in that fancy bathroom while he was waiting.

After a few moments, Sonya looked up at her visitor and smiled. "Now, Mr. Morris, how may I help you?"

"I'm concerned about Miss Hannah," Bradley said, his tone blunt and to the point.

Sonya raised her hands in mock helplessness. "And so am I, Mr. Morris. She hasn't come in, and she hasn't contacted me."

And you look awfully happy about it, Bradley thought. "That's what I mean, Miss Colby. That's not at all like Vel, uh, Miss Hannah," he corrected himself.

Sonya smirked and looked at Bradley curiously. "Are you and Miss Hannah friendly, Mr. Morris?"

"Oh, no. I just knew her before she became one of the owners of the agency."

"I see." Sonya looked at him for a moment. *I wonder how well he knew her*, she thought. "What can I say? I certainly don't know where she is."

"She would never just stay away without a word."

"She's doing just that, Mr. Morris."

"No, I'm telling you, she wouldn't. Something is wrong. I think you should send the police, or at least security, out to her place to check on her."

Sonya's face clouded. "Are you trying to tell me how to do my job, Mr. Morris?"

"Of course, not, Miss Colby. I just think time is of the essence here. As I said, this is unusual for Miss Hannah."

Sonya forced a smile. "I'm sorry. I'm afraid I don't know her as well as you do, Mr. Morris. But, if it will ease your mind, I've already notified security. We have everything under control."

"They're going to check on her then?" Bradley's voice was hopeful.

"First thing in the morning, if we haven't heard from her by then."

Bradley was incredulous. "You're going to wait another day?"

"Look, Mr. Morris, maybe she's just tired and wanted to get away for a while. God knows she deserves it after I just disappeared on her for four years. Maybe she wants me to see what it's like having to carry the agency all by myself. Maybe I deserve to be taught a lesson. I have no idea what this is all about, but if she does want privacy for a while, I'd hate to spoil that for her. Let me handle this, please."

"All right, Miss Colby. Maybe you're right, but I still think this is out of character for Miss Hannah."

"Of course, I'm right. She has been working awfully hard."

Bradley rose. "Thank you for your time."

"You're welcome, Mr. Morris. Feel free to come see me anytime."

"Thank you." Bradley turned and left the office.

He was not convinced.

Sonya looked at her watch. She had to hurry. All the interruptions, and all of them about Velma Hannah. She gathered her things and went out into the front office. "I'm going to lunch, Ms. Odom, then I have a few appointments, so I might not make it back to the office this afternoon. Mr. Simms will be here if there's a problem."

"Yes, Miss Colby," Lisa said. "Have a good lunch."

"Thank you." Sonya left the office. A wry smile played on her lips.

***

Tom Simms was enjoying the second day of Velma Hannah's absence from The William E. Colby Agency. He sat behind the desk in Velma's office now. He felt good just sitting there, not just in a corner office, but in the most prestigious office at the agency.

He looked about the room and thought about how he would redecorate it. He looked at the white, antique desk, closed his eyes, and envisioned his seven-drawer, solid oak, executive desk in its place.

This thought brought a smile to his face. He had talked William Colby into having the desk shipped out from the west coast. Yes, it would look awfully nice in this big, spacious office. Of course, he would have the color scheme changed before moving in his furniture. He looked about the room and chuckled to himself.

Women. What odd tastes they have, he thought.

Then a dreadful thought occurred to him. Suppose Sonya decided she wanted this office. Surely she wouldn't—not after just having hers redecorated. But, then, he knew that no one could predict what Sonya was going to do from one minute to the next.

Then an even more dreadful thought hit him. Suppose Velma Hannah returned. Where was she? For an instant, while talking with Sonya the day before, he had a feeling she knew something about the woman's disappearance.

Sonya is devious. I think she knows something, but I'll be darned if I'll open my mouth—not when I'm about to achieve my lifelong dream of heading up this agency, he thought.

Neither of the women, the former owner had put in charge, knew as much as he did about the business. He was the proper person to run it. Maybe somebody upstairs was looking out for him after all. He would take his blessings anyway he could get them.

Tom leaned back in Velma Hannah's chair and smiled. "Tom Simms, your ship is finally coming into port," he said to himself, a broad smile spreading across his face.

CHAPTER 22

The old woman stood in front of the mirror in the late Claire Gene Colby's bedroom. She wore many pieces of jewelry. They were about her neck, pinned to her clothes, on her ears, her wrists, and on her fingers. The picture that covered the safe on the wall was on the floor. The safe stood open. The woman smiled broadly as she admired herself in the mirror.

"My jewelry," she whispered. "I've got my jewelry back."

Callie could not believe her good fortune.

Velma had been listening. She had not heard a sound from the man in the other room in what seemed like an awfully long time. She wondered if he were dead or alive. She decided to try to arouse him.

"Hello in there," she yelled. "Hello! Mister? Mister?"

"What do you want, lady?" came the weak reply.

"My name is Velma Hannah. Who are you?"

"I know who you are, lady. I know all about you."

Of course, he would know about her. She hated to think about the things he had heard. "I see. But...who are you?"

"My name is Harry Reynolds. I was the Colby's chauffeur."

Velma thought for a moment. "Yes, William, I mean Mr. Colby, used to talk about you."

"Did he tell you his daughter and I had a thing going on?" He chuckled.

"No." Velma paused a moment. "How...? Why are you here?"

"Just lucky, I guess," was Harry's flippant reply.

A moment of silence passed, then Velma decided to question him further.

"Why did she bring you down here?"

"To show me she hadn't killed you."

"Then you came here looking for me?"

"No, Miss Hannah, I'm afraid I was looking for something else."

"But why—?" Velma began.

"You ask a lot of questions, lady."

Was he in on this with Sonya? What was his connection? She had to know. "How did you know I was here?"

"I saw you come here Saturday night. I also knew you never left."

"Then why didn't you call the police for goodness sake?"

"I had other plans. Unfortunately, they didn't pan out."

Velma had her answer. If things had gone the man's way, she would still be Sonya's prisoner—the only one. "I see. But now that we're in this together, we must do something."

"And what would you suggest? You want me to turn into Super Man?" His voice was sarcastic.

"How does she have you tied?"

"To a chair. An oversized one."

Velma thought for a moment. "Can you slide it?"

There was a long silence.

"It's too heavy," he finally said, sounding out of breath.

"Try!" Velma screamed.

"What do you think I've been doing for the last five minutes?" he screamed back.

"Then try harder. If you can get out here, I can untie you!"

Harry struggled trying to move the heavy chair that seemed glued to the floor. Finally, it moved a smidgen. "It moved!" he yelled.

"Great," Velma yelled back. "Oh, thank you, God," she whispered. "Keep sliding it!" .

"I'm trying," was Harry's reply.

Velma sat anxiously waiting. After what seemed like an eternity, she called to him again, "What are you doing?"

"This chair's too heavy. I just can't move it," Harry said.

"You must!"

"I'm doing my best, lady."

"You have to get out here! You have to! It's our only chance to free ourselves!"

"I can only move it a fraction of an inch at a time."

"Then keep moving it that fraction! And hurry, for God's sake!"

"I'm doing the best I can!" His voice was angry.

A few minutes later, she heard him bump the door.

He made it, she thought. "Open the door!" she yelled.

"I can just touch it with the toe of my shoe. My arms are tied down. I can move them just to my elbows, and my feet are tied, too!" Harry yelled back.

Velma thought for a moment. "Maneuver the side of the chair around to the door, so you can use your hands!"

"I'm trying," Harry said. After a few moments, he continued, "I can't turn this chair around. It might tip over!"

"You've got to turn it around! You've got to! We'll both die down here if you don't!"

"I can't perform miracles, lady!"

"My name is Velma, Harry. Velma. And I know you can't perform miracles, but please try to turn that chair so you can reach the doorknob with your hands."

Another lengthy silence followed with intermittent bumping sounds coming from the other room. Finally, Harry spoke. "I just can't do it...Velma!"

"Try tilting the chair to the side," Velma urged.

"If I tilt this chair anymore, I'm going to land on the floor!"

"There has to be a way."

"Well, I'm tired of trying. I've got to rest."

Velma was totally unnerved. "There's no time to rest! You must concentrate on getting free!"

"You're not in here pushing this chair around! I am!"

"Look, Harry," Velma said helplessly, "if we don't help ourselves, we're both going to die. I certainly can't break these chains, but I could untie you if you could only get out here where I am."

"I'm trying." He sounded completely frustrated.

Velma sighed. "I'm sorry. I know you are. Do the best you can."

She bowed her head and began to pray.

CHAPTER 23

Sonya's car pulled up in front of the condominium complex. *The perfect place for an illicit love affair*, she thought.

She remembered the place well. She had sat out in front of the building many nights watching Velma Hannah and her father coming and going. They were happy. So happy, while she and her mother, his wife, were living a life of hell.

Sonya pulled on a pair of gloves, took Velma's keys from her purse, and got out of the car. She went swiftly to the front entrance and tried a few keys before finding the one that unlocked the security door. She went inside the building and closed the door behind her. So much for the guard on duty. His station just inside the entrance was empty. She didn't even have to tell the wonderful lie she had concocted.

Sonya took the elevator to the tenth floor. She was grateful for the middle of the day. The place seemed deserted. The guard and everybody else must have been out to lunch.

They should be more careful at an exclusive complex like this, she thought.

Sonya got off the elevator and walked down the hallway checking the numbers on the doors as she passed them. She stopped in front of ten twenty-one. After trying a few keys, the lock on the door clicked. Sonya opened the door and stepped inside. As she was closing the door, Geronimo came bounding into the room. He raced up to her.

"Why hello, Geronimo," she cooed.

Geronimo stopped short at the sight of the strange woman.

"Oh, you thought I was your mommy," Sonya said bending down, smiling at the cat. Then she threw back her head and began to laugh.

Geronimo turned and ran.

Sonya raced after him. "Come back, kitty." She stopped in the hallway, looking about for the cat.

Geronimo was nowhere to be found.

"Where did the little shit go?" Sonya asked herself. Then she noticed the door to a room standing ajar. She went into the room.

Her bedroom. How nice. Is this where my daddy got his thrills? she thought

After searching the room for a possible hiding place, Sonya decided the cat must have gone under the bed. She got down on her hands and knees beside the bed and looked under it. Sure enough, there he was, his eyes gleaming in the darkness.

"Come on, kitty," Sonya said trying to coax the cat out from under the bed.

Geronimo stood his ground. He just sat, glaring at her.

"Come on out, Geronimo. I'm not going to hurt you." Sonya reached her hand under the bed.

Geronimo scratched her.

"Ouch!" She jerked back her hand. "You little bastard!" she screamed, when she saw blood beginning to ooze from several scratches on her hand.

She jumped up and raced from the room. She found a broom in the kitchen closet and brought it back to the bedroom. She got down on her hands and knees beside the bed and began thrashing under it with the broom.

Geronimo raced past her out the door. Sonya ran after him, closing the door behind her.

She found him at the front door meowing to be let out. She stood, surveying the situation for a moment. She knew her chances of getting close enough to hit the cat with the broom were nil. She spotted a silver candlestick on a table nearby. She picked up the gleaming piece of silver.

"Nice and heavy," she whispered to herself.

Sonya threw the candlestick, and it caught Geronimo on the side of the head. He fell. Sonya ran over to him. He struggled trying to get to his feet, but Sonya was too fast for him. She picked up the weapon and struck the cat again and again until his struggling ceased. She looked down on Geronimo for a moment, then smiled, pleased with her accomplishment. She put the candlestick back on the table.

Sonya took the broom back to the kitchen then got a garbage bag from a box under the sink. She went back into the living room, picked up the lifeless cat, and put him in the bag.

Minutes later, she put the bag with Geronimo's lifeless body in the trunk of her car, went around to the driver's side, opened the door, got in, and drove off down the street.

Velma sat looking in awe at the shelled peas that sat beside her in the pan on the floor. She had worked until her eyes had become so droopy she could not keep them open any longer. At some point, she had fallen asleep. When she awoke, several hours later, most of the peas had been shelled.

"The woman," she whispered. "She's trying to help me. Who is she?" *Why doesn't she help me get free*? she thought. Surely she knew the man was there, too. Did they dare hope?

"Harry?" she called.

"Yes?" came the weak reply from the other room.

"Did you see the woman? Did she come in there?" Her voice was hopeful, anxious.

"What are you talking about, lady, uh, Velma?"

"There's someone else in the house, Harry. A woman."

"You're crazy."

"No. She was down here in the basement. I fell asleep, and she helped me with my work."

"Look Velma, I didn't see nobody. This is getting to you."

"No, Harry. She shelled some of the peas while I was sleeping."

"Maybe you dreamed it."

"I didn't! She was here last night, also. She washed my back and put something on my wounds. I forgot to tell you before."

"Sure," Harry said dryly. "While you were dreaming, I was tilting this chair. I almost knocked my brains out on that door. I've finally got it upright again, and I'm going to leave it that way."

"You're giving up?"

"I've got no choice! You send your phantom in here the next time she appears. Let her untie me."

He doesn't believe me, Velma thought. Well, so much for that. Then she wondered if their plan had been successful, and she had freed the man, if he would have hung around long enough to try to help her, or even brought back the police.

Somehow, Velma did not think so.

She would have to try to get through to the woman. That seemed to be their only hope. The woman was apparently hiding in the house, and Sonya had not discovered her yet. A homeless person? How had she gotten into the house? How long had she been here? What would Sonya do if she found out about her?

Velma flinched when she thought about what Sonya might do to the woman if she were to discover her presence. How was this person managing to avoid contact with Sonya?

"She's using her head," Velma whispered to herself. *She's thinking, and that means she can be reasoned with*, she thought. She had to make the woman understand that she had to get help for her and the man.

And Velma, once again, dared to hope.

CHAPTER 24

Bradley Morris had neglected his work, and staff, during the past two days. In spite of himself, he could not help but worry about the disappearance of his employer. The woman stayed on his mind night and day. The thought of something bad happening to her sent unexplained chills through his body. He had decided, near the end of the second workday, that he could not wait for others to act. He was going to Velma's place to check on her.

He picked up the telephone and dialed information.

Sonya hurried home. She parked the car in the garage and took the bag with Geronimo's body out of the trunk. She went straight to the kitchen. She was excited, could not wait to see Velma's face. She chuckled as she set the bag on the floor beside the sink.

She looked down at the bag. "Meow," she said and began to laugh.

Bradley Morris stood in the office of the Audabon Management Association, the company that managed Velma's condominium complex. He had been talking with the person in charge for several minutes now trying to get her to realize the seriousness of the situation at hand so she would accompany him to Velma's place. He was finally beginning to make some headway.

The woman thought for a moment longer then nodded her head. "All right, Mr. Morris, I'll go with you."

She turned to a woman who sat at another desk in the office. "Verlillian, I'll be back in a few minutes."

Verlillian waved a hand, indicating that she had heard, and kept on with her work.

Bradley sighed with relief.

Velma heard the door at the top of the stairs open. Then the lights were on. *It's late*, Velma thought. She had heard Sonya come in hours ago. What had she been doing all that time? She heard footsteps on the stairs. Then Sonya was standing over her, smiling down on her, holding a huge, covered tray in her hands.

Sonya looked at the pan of peas. "I see you were a good girl today. You did all of your work. Very good. For that, I'm going to reward you. Here's a nice, hot tray of food for your dinner. I cooked it myself. Special. I hope you like it." She lifted the lid a bit and held the tray down so Velma could smell the food. "Doesn't it smell delightful?"

It does, Velma thought. "Yes," she said. "Thank you."

"My pleasure."

Velma did not know what to think. Could it really be true? Was Sonya actually giving her something decent to eat? Did she dare hope?

With a flourish, Sonya set the tray on the floor beside Velma and uncovered it. "Fried Geronimo!" she shouted, and laughed, and laughed, and laughed.

Velma looked at the tray in horror. Geronimo's head sat in the middle of it. His huge green eyes were open, and they seemed to be staring straight at her. All around the head were pieces of meat—chopped, battered, and fried to perfection. *The rest of his body*, Velma thought.

She fainted.

Sonya laughed until she cried. Then she went back up the stairs. In a few minutes, she returned with another tray. On it were a slice of bread and two glasses of water. She stopped momentarily looking down on the still unconscious Velma. She threw the water from one of the glasses in Velma's face. In a moment, Velma stirred then opened her eyes.

Sonya chuckled. "I see you didn't like your dinner. Tut, tut. What a shame. Well, that's all you're going to get tonight. Eat the kitty or starve."

Velma pulled herself up to a sitting position and pushed the tray away from her. "My God," she whispered, her voice tearful. She looked up at Sonya. "How could you do such a thing?"

"It was easy." Sonya began to laugh again. Then she turned and went on into Harry's room.

Harry had moved his chair back to its original position. It would not be wise to arouse suspicion. Sliding it over to the door had been a futile effort anyway. There was no sense in adding fuel to the already flaming fire.

"Well, looks like you've been a good boy today, too, Harry. Here's your dinner. I hope you enjoy it."

She set the tray on Harry's lap. He did not knock it off this time. He grabbed the piece of bread and, in two bites, it was gone. He washed it down with the glass of water. Sonya stood over her prey enjoying the scene before her.

"Can I have some more, Sonya? Please," Harry pleaded.

"May I have some more?" Sonya said, correcting his grammar.

"This is no time for an English lesson! You're starving me!" Harry shouted.

"That's exactly what I plan to do, Harry. In answer to your question, no, you may not have more. Your next meal will be at breakfast if you're a good boy tonight, that is."

Beads of perspiration began to pop out on Harry's forehead. "Sonya, let's make a deal," he pleaded.

"You're in no position to make deals, Harry."

"Please! I'll do anything."

"You, Harry, will do nothing ever again but stay here in this room until you rot. Everything was going beautifully until you interrupted. Greed, Harry. You're suffering from a severe case of greed, and sometimes greed will kill you quicker than cancer. My mother left you ten thousand dollars. But that wasn't enough for you, was it? But, then, I guess that's life. Some people never get enough. Some just keep trying to get something for nothing, and some even kill themselves trying. Greed is a real killer, Harry."

"Sonya, this is insane. You'll have to at least untie me, so I can go to the bathroom."

"Hold it, Harry, until I've figured out what to do about that matter. I didn't expect more than one guest, and she has access to the only bathroom down here. Your being an uninvited guest is a problem for both of us."

"I can't just sit here day after day and..." Harry left the sentence dangling.

"Then perhaps I should cut down on your food. If you don't eat or drink, there won't be anything to eliminate. Right, Harry?"

Harry was dumbfounded. He simply stared at her.

"Hold it, Harry, until I give you permission to do otherwise." Sonya took the tray, turned, went out the door, and slammed it behind her.

"Sonya! Sonya, come back! Sonyyyyyyya!"

Sonya walked past Velma and on up the stairs. She turned out the lights, and slammed the door behind her, Harry's voice still ringing in her ears.

Harry finally stopped calling to Sonya. He dropped his head to his chest and sobbed.

Sonya went on up to the second floor to her bedroom. She was tired. It had taken her a long time to cut off the cat's head and skin his body. Then she had to chop it, batter it, and wait for it to cook. But it had all been worth it. The look on Velma's face had made it all worthwhile.

She moved over in front of the mirror and began to undress. *I should have removed my clothes*, she thought. There were bloodstains on the front of her suit. She would have to burn it. She had been so involved with what she was doing and the thought of making Velma Hannah squirm, she had completely forgotten to change. She was more than pleased with her performance, though.

She smiled at her reflection in the mirror.

Her smile instantly faded and she began to glare into the mirror, her eyes wide. Her hand went automatically to the spot on her jacket where she had pinned the jade brooch that morning. She panicked. The brooch was gone. She looked about her on the floor.

"No," she whispered. "My brooch. Where's my brooch?"

She ran out into the hallway and retraced her steps. She hurried back downstairs to the kitchen and looked frantically about on the floor. *Maybe it fell off in the basement*, she thought.

But her search of the basement proved futile also. All she had done down there was to further frighten her guests.

But maybe that was a good thing.

Then she remembered her fight with the cat. "That's it," she said to herself. "It probably fell off at Velma's place. I have to go back." She was furious.

But how would she get past the guard? He was probably not so lax this time of day. She had to think—and fast.

Sonya ran back up the stairs to her bedroom and quickly changed clothes. A few minutes later, she sped off down the street in her car.

There were police cars all over the place outside Velma's condominium. The police were everywhere, and spectators were standing about. Bradley Morris and the lady from the Audabon Management Association were among them. They both had been questioned, and Bradley had told them all he knew about Velma's disappearance.

Blood samples from a silver candlestick and the carpet at the front door were being sent to the lab. A jade brooch, that had been found on the floor beside Velma's bed, was also being held as evidence.

Bradley was totally unnerved. The thought of Velma being hurt, possibly dead, left him weak. He prodded his memory trying to remember where he had seen that brooch. On whom? And recently. He tried to picture, in his mind, the outfits Velma had worn to work the week before. He had a good memory, but he could not recall the brooch on her. It seemed too recent.

"Is there anything else you can tell us, Mr. Morris?" one of the policemen asked.

"No, I've told you all I know," Bradley said. His thoughts still raced.

"Then I guess we're finished here." The officer turned to another man beside him. "Round up the men, Collins."

"Yes, sir," Collins said and walked away.

Sonya turned her car around when she saw all the commotion outside the condominium complex.

Someone must have been snooping around where they had no business and called the police, she thought. Or maybe they were there for some other reason. But she could not take any chances. If the brooch was there, and they found it, they would assume it was Velma's. No, she had nothing about which to worry. Nothing. She had been careful. Tonight, she would sleep soundly.

Velma opened her eyes. How long had she been asleep? She saw light. Someone had turned on the lamp across the room. Then she saw the blurred figure of someone standing over her.

"Hello," she whispered.

The person moved away. The light went out, and the figure went toward the stairs.

It's the woman, Velma thought. "Come back," she said. "Please don't go. Help us. Please. Come back."

The woman went on up the stairs, and Velma heard the door close quietly behind her.

CHAPTER 25

The noise was coming closer. It was a shrill. A woman's voice. No, a man's. It was both. But what were they saying? Velma sat up with a start. Someone was laughing—a woman. And a man was saying something. She realized the sound was coming from Harry's room. The light was on and the woman was standing in the doorway. Her hair was disheveled, and her clothes hung loosely on her body. She was looking into the room, laughing, and Harry was shouting at her.

"Callie, untie me! Untie me, Callie! Help me! Please, Callie!"

Callie, Velma thought. Did Harry know the woman?

The woman turned out the light and closed the door.

"No, Callie! Come back! Please, Callie!" Harry's frantic voice continued.

The woman turned, still laughing. Velma strained her eyes trying to get a look at her. It was too dark. She could not see her facial features.

The woman rushed past Velma toward the stairs.

"Come back! Come back! Callie?" Velma's voice joined Harry's calling to the woman.

The woman stopped laughing momentarily. She turned, and looked at Velma.

"Call the police. Please! Get help for me and the man. We need help," Velma pleaded.

The woman turned back around and went hurriedly up the stairs, her laughter fresh and anew.

"Get the police!" Velma shouted after the fleeing woman. "Please, call the police!"

She heard the door at the top of the stairs close and the woman's laughter fade.

"Harry!" Velma called.

"Yes?" Harry answered, his voice listless.

"Now you know I was telling the truth."

"Yes. She was the Colby's maid."

"Then you do know her? I heard you call her Callie."

"Yes, her name is Callie Foster. She looks much older—and wild. But it's Callie all right. I'd know her anywhere. We both worked here for years. She's crazy. Has completely lost her mind. Did you see her eyes?"

"No," Velma said. "I couldn't. What is she doing here?"

"I have no idea. Sonya let us all go the same day. Callie must have come back, or she never left. I don't know."

Velma remembered the night she had come by the house right after Sonya left town, over four years earlier, and the maid—yes, the woman said she was the maid—had answered the door. Velma had gone to see the lawyer the next day, and he had told her all the servants had been dismissed. She had thought it strange.

Could it be that the maid never left?

"My God. Has she been in this house all that time?" Velma whispered to herself. "She's trying to help!" Velma said to Harry. "Why didn't she untie you? Why was she laughing, for God's sake?"

"Callie and I never got along. I guess you could say we hated each other."

"She refused to untie you?"

"You saw what she did. She's mad. We can't depend on a crazy woman to help us."

"But she is trying to help."

"You, maybe, but not me."

There has to be a way to get to her, Velma thought. The woman was smart enough to be staying here in the

184

house without getting caught, and she remembered Harry and that he was not a friend. There was hope. Velma refused to believe otherwise.

"Harry?" she called.

"Yes, Velma, what is it now?"

"What do you know about Callie Foster?"

"Nothing. She was just another Black maid. I've seen many of them."

"Just another Black maid." Velma's voice was filled with irony.

"That's right. She did her job, and I did mine."

Like, maybe a machine, Velma thought. No character. No notable attributes worth remembering. "No wonder she didn't untie you!" she yelled.

"What's that supposed to mean?" Harry asked.

"Think about it."

Velma was tired and sleepy. She forced herself to stay awake at night while Sonya was in the house. She never knew what to expect from the girl. She felt safer sleeping during the day while her captor was away.

I must have fallen asleep right after Sonya left this morning, she thought.

She had eaten the slice of bread and drunk the water. Then she had shelled a few of the peas. The peas. She had to stay awake at least long enough to shell the peas. Then she would sleep the rest of the day.

Velma went back to her work.

So he's the one, Sonya thought. She sat behind the desk in her office. Bradley Morris, visibly agitated, sat on a chair in front of it. Sonya wanted to do something bad to this man who was obviously in love with the woman she wanted more than anything to destroy.

"The manager and I called the police," Bradley said.

"I see." Sonya had managed a sufficient amount of shock, interest, and concern at the story Bradley Morris had just told her. "That's most distressing news, Mr. Morris. Of course, you know she and I weren't the best of friends, but we did have an amicable working relationship. I'd certainly hate to have anyone affiliated with the agency become the victim of some kind of foul play."

"The blood was fairly fresh. We should have checked on her sooner."

"I'm sorry," Sonya said. This man was on her nerves—badly. She was tired of trying to be civil to him. But he was smart, and if she blew up on him now, he might suspect her of having something to do with Velma's disappearance—if he hadn't already. She could not let that happen. Since he seemed to like playing detective so much, he might accidentally stumble onto something the police could not ignore.

Calm yourself, Sonya, she thought. "I just didn't want to interfere. I had no idea..." Sonya left the sentence dangling.

Bradley stared at her, an uncanny look on his face.

"What's wrong, Mr. Morris?" she asked. *The man is beside himself*, she thought.

She wondered how long he had been smitten with the Black wench. Perhaps he did not know the requirements upon which the lady granted her favors. In his case, a bleach job first. Then there would be the matter of money, of course.

"Nothing. Nothing," Bradley said, his mind obviously preoccupied. "Of course, you couldn't have known." He rose. "I've taken enough of your time. I'll get back to work and let you do the same. We'll just let the police do their job now."

"Yes. That's about all we can do, Mr. Morris."

"Thank you for seeing me." Bradley turned and started hurriedly from the office.

"Oh, Mr. Morris," Sonya called after him.

Bradley turned back to her. "Yes, Miss Colby?"

"Let's not alarm the rest of the staff just yet. Why don't we let this remain between the two of us until we hear further from the police as to what has really happened to Miss Hannah?"

"Maybe you're right," Bradley said. He left the office, closing the door quietly behind him.

Sonya looked after him. She was angry. She stared at the closed door for a few moments, her eyes wild. Then she leaped to her feet, snatched up the telephone from the desk and slammed it to the floor.

Lisa was in the doorway instantly, a look of alarm on her face. "Is everything all right, Miss Colby?"

Sonya bent down and picked up the telephone. "Yes, Ms. Odom. Just clumsiness, I'm afraid. I knocked the telephone off the desk."

"Oh." Lisa smiled and went back into her office.

Bradley went down the hallway berating himself. How could he have forgotten? Sonya had worn that jade brooch only the day before. He had noticed it when he went in to talk with her about Velma. On a light green suit. *Most becoming*, he had thought. He had always admired rich women and the way they dressed.

Yes, he was sure of it, and that meant Sonya had been in Velma's house. That also meant his hunch was right: the woman was involved in Velma's disappearance—maybe her death.

He had to get to the police. But would they believe him or William Colby's daughter? It would just be his word against hers, and what kind of pull did he have in Baltonville? None, to be exact. They would laugh him right out of the precinct. If they didn't, that lawyer of hers would surely crucify him.

She's putting on a most convincing act, he thought. It would be difficult trying to prove his suspicions. And if he were successful in getting someone to listen to him, by that time, it would probably be too late to help Velma—if, in fact, she was still alive.

No, he had to find her, and he had to do it on his own.

Bradley stopped outside his office door for a moment as the thought hit him that his life could also be in danger. He knew now for a fact that Sonya Ellis Colby was a dangerous woman.

***

Bradley sat in his office, on the twenty-fourth floor of The William E. Colby Agency, thinking. He couldn't even pretend to work. His thoughts were too full of Velma Hannah—of a plan that was forming in his mind.

A memo, circulated the day before, stated that Sonya was meeting with account executives at two o'clock. He had seen her put her keys in her top desk drawer when he was in her office earlier. He had to get those keys and have duplicates made while she was in that meeting. He just hoped she hadn't taken them with her.

If I can get into her house, I might find something that would be of help, he thought. But he had to get past her secretary first.

Bradley checked his watch. It was one-fifty. He had to do some fast thinking. Lisa was probably still in the conference room seeing that all preparations for the meeting were complete: company pads and pens for everyone to pretend to take notes—and refreshments, of course. Eating made people more agreeable, he guessed.

Lisa would probably stay there until Sonya arrived then return to the office—if she followed the usual procedure at The William E. Colby Agency, that is. Of course, Sonya might change company policy to suit herself anytime.

He would take his chances.

Bradley surveyed the activity in his department. The place was buzzing. Everyone was hard at work—producing.

Nice, he thought. Everyone was working but the boss who had business that, at the moment, was more important. "Personal?" he asked himself out loud.

Maybe.

A few minutes later, Bradley stood in the hallway on the twenty-fifth floor, waiting, surreptitiously watching Sonya's office door. If she or Lisa came out of the office, he would pretend to be leaving the executive lounge that was directly across the hall. If anyone came out of the lounge, he would pretend to be going inside.

Bradley had been at his post only a couple of minutes when the office door opened, and Sonya came through it. She went down the hallway in the opposite direction. She rounded the corner, and Bradley hurried down the hallway to her office. He opened the door, and, sure enough, the secretary's office was empty. He went into Sonya's private office, walked over to the desk, and opened the center drawer.

He was in luck. The keys were there, right where he had seen her put them. He picked up the ring of keys, put them in his pocket, closed the desk drawer, and hurried from the office. Just as he closed the door to Sonya's office, Lisa came through the outside door into her office.

She looked at Bradley, startled for a moment. "Oh, Mr. Morris. May I help you?"

Bradley flashed a big smile. "I was looking for Miss Colby. You weren't in, so I knocked on her door. When she didn't answer, I peeked inside. But I see she's not in at the moment."

"No, she's in a meeting."

"Of course. The two o'clock with accounting." Bradley slapped his forehead, indicating that he had forgotten.

"Yes. May I give her a message?"

"No. No, I'll come back later. Thank you." Bradley left the office. He closed the door behind him and emitted a long sigh of relief.

"Close call," he whispered. He hurried to the elevator and punched the down button. *There's a key shop just around the corner*, he thought. He could have duplicates made and still be back in plenty of time to return Sonya's keys to her desk drawer. But he would have to think of a way to get past Lisa, the hawk.

A few minutes later, Bradley walked into the key shop, and his hopes fell. "Jeez," he whispered. *Did everybody in Baltonville lose his spare key today?* he thought. Well, what else could he do?

He got in line.

CHAPTER 26

Velma awoke and was startled to see that the lamp had been turned on. *Sonya's home already?* she thought. She had dozed off again, but she could not have slept too long. She had gotten so tired shelling the peas. Then she noticed the peas she had left in the basket were now shelled and in the pan.

"The woman," she whispered. She looked hurriedly about the room. Then her eyes fell on a small tray beside her on the floor. It held a bowl of soup, a sandwich, a cup of tea, and a wet face towel. Velma felt the bowl. The soup was still warm. She looked about the room again trying to at least get a glimpse of the mysterious woman.

Nothing.

Velma turned back to the tray. She took the towel and wiped her hands and face. The cool, damp cloth felt so refreshing to her skin. She wanted to take a bath so badly, but because the chains only allowed her to go as far into the bathroom as the toilet stool, she would have to be content with wash-ups in the face bowl.

"Harry," she called.

"Yes?" came Harry's dry reply.

"Callie was back down here. Did she come in there?"

"No." Harry's voice was eager. "She came back?"

"Yes, she finished my work for me, and," she paused, hating to tell him, "she brought me some food."

"What?" Harry could not believe what he had just heard. "She brought you something to eat?"

"Yes, and I'm sorry I can't share it with you, Harry. But you see she is trying to help me. I don't know what the problem was between the two of you, but you've got to try to make amends with her. She's our only hope."

"But she's out of her mind. I can tell just by looking at her. She doesn't know what she's doing."

"She does, Harry. I'm telling you, she does." Velma's voice was desperate.

Harry was an irritating individual. "She just brought me some food, because she knows I'm hungry. And she helped me with my work, because she knows Sonya will hurt me if I don't have it done when she gets home."

"All right. All right. If she's really trying to help you, then I guess she knows we're in trouble." Harry's voice was not too convincing.

"That's right. I'm doing all I can, but you're going to have to help. She could untie you, but she certainly can't break these chains!" Velma almost screamed at him.

"I know, Velma. You don't have to get mad about it."

"We're in a life or death situation here, Harry. I see a glimmer of hope, and I'm grasping for it."

"I hope you're right. But I don't see anyway out of this. At least you won't starve to death."

"I'm sorry."

"Yeah," Harry said.

Velma laid the towel beside her on the floor and turned to the food on the tray. "Thank you, Lord," she whispered.

She felt sorry for Harry, but, right now, she was hungry, and she was going to eat. *Slowly*, she thought. She had heard that a near starving person should eat slowly. Chew well. She would do her best.

She bowed her head, said a blessing over the first real meal she had had since her ordeal began, and then tasted the soup. It was split pea and so good.

Velma thanked God for the woman, as demented as she might be.

Bradley rushed back to the office building. He went past the guard then literally ran down the corridor to the elevators. He had waited in line all of forty-five minutes to have the duplicate keys made—and then she had so many. He had ruled out five that could not possibly be house keys. That left seven to be duplicated. And the duplicating had taken much longer than it should have. It was just his luck to go in on a day when a new employee was being trained. In all, he had been gone an hour and five minutes.

Much too long, he thought. He looked at his watch then punched the up elevator button. His only hope was that Sonya was as long winded as her father had been when conducting meetings.

Bradley entered Sonya's office. Lisa looked up. "Miss Colby just came in," she said. "I'll tell her you're here, Mr. Morris."

Bradley was crushed. He had not made it. Now what? *All those people*, he thought.

What could he say?

"Thank you, Ms. Odom." What would he say he wanted with the woman? He had to think of something.

Lisa picked up the telephone and punched a button. "Mr. Morris is here to see you, Miss Colby." In a moment, she replaced the receiver, and looked up at Bradley. "You may go in."

"Thank you," Bradley said. His mind raced. He had to think of some ruse—and fast. He opened the door to Sonya's private office, entered the spacious, elaborately decorated room, and then closed the door behind him.

"I'm glad you're here, Mr. Morris," Sonya said. "Please sit down."

Bradley sat on a chair in front of Sonya's desk. Maybe his problem was solved. It appeared that the lady wanted to see him.

"I believe the big mystery has been solved," Sonya continued.

Bradley looked at her, a bewildered expression on his face. She held up the letter she had forced Velma to write the day before.

"The mail came while I was in my meeting. This letter, marked personal, was on my desk when I returned to my office. It's from Miss Hannah. I'd like for you to read it. Of course, I'll have to show it to the police."

"A letter?" Bradley stood. *The keys*, he thought. He had to get them back into her desk drawer. Then he saw it, a cup of coffee, sitting on the edge of the desk. *God, I hope it's not hot*, he thought. He reached for the letter his hand brushing the side of the cup. The cup fell and landed on Sonya's lap.

"Aaaaah! You clumsy fool!" Sonya leaped to her feet, brushing frantically at the front of her clothes.

Bradley, immobilized for a second, sprang into action. He raced around the desk apologizing profusely. "I'm so sorry." He pulled a handkerchief from his pocket and started to brush at Sonya's skirt. "Here, let me help you."

"Keep your hands off me," Sonya hissed. She hurried across the office and disappeared into her private bathroom.

Bradley opened the desk drawer and reached into his pocket for the keys.

Lisa came through the door. "What's all the commotion in here?"

Bradley bent on down to the floor and picked up the coffee cup. "An accident," he said. He set the cup on the desk. "I'm afraid I spilled coffee on her dress."

Lisa looked at him in stunned silence for a moment. She could not believe this worrisome, clumsy idiot. "You spilled coffee on her clothes?"

Before Bradley could answer, Lisa hurried into Sonya's bathroom.

Bradley was thankful for small favors. He pulled the ring of keys from his pocket, put them in the drawer, closed the drawer, then picked up the letter from Sonya's desk, and began to read it. As he read, his expression changed from one of awe to one of disbelief.

Bradley was pacing the floor in front of Sonya's desk, the letter still open in his hand, when the two angry women emerged from the bathroom.

"I'll have to go home," Sonya snapped.

"I'm so sorry, Miss Colby." Lisa's angry eyes came to rest on Bradley's face.

"So am I," Bradley said. "Of course, I'll pay for the cleaning."

"That won't be necessary," Sonya said. "Did you read the letter?"

"Yes, and I can't believe this." Bradley waved the letter through the air.

"I can, Mr. Morris. It's quite explicit. Now if you will excuse me." Sonya got her handbag from a bottom drawer of her desk then grabbed her keys from the top middle drawer, and started for the door. "Please leave the letter on my desk." She left the office.

Bradley laid the letter on the desk and followed her out the door. Lisa brought up the rear.

CHAPTER 27

The sandwich had been some kind of meat spread, and it was delicious. Velma sat finishing up her tea when her mysterious friend came running down the stairs.

Callie had changed her clothes. She was now formally attired. Her clothes were dated but looked expensive. She wore a black, off-the-shoulder sheath gown with a split up the front. On her feet were black, high-heeled, satin pumps. On her hands were many rings. She wore a gold watch on one wrist and a diamond bracelet on the other. About her neck was a pearl necklace of multiple strands.

She had made an attempt to style her completely gray hair in an upsweep on top of her head. Strands of hair hung loose, stuck out on the sides, in the back, and on top of her head.

Callie raced up to Velma, snatched the cup from her hand, and put it on the tray beside Velma on the floor. Then she grabbed the tray, raced over and turned out the lamp, and ran back up the stairs.

"No, wait! Wait!" Velma shouted after the fleeing woman.

Callie continued up the stairs.

"Callie, get the keys so you can unlock the chains! Please help me!" Velma continued. She heard the door at the top of the stairs close.

Velma sat in wonderment. What was wrong? Why had Callie been in such a rush? Her dress. Velma had seen it before. She had also gotten a pretty good look at the woman's face when she bent down to take the cup from her hand. Deeply wrinkled. Aged prematurely? And her eyes were completely wild.

Is my potential savior as mad as my captor? Velma thought.

Perhaps Harry was right.

The door at the top of the stairs opened, and Velma dared to hope again, even against the odds. *She's coming back*, she thought.

The lights went on, and Velma heard footsteps on the stairs.

"Help me, please," Velma said, her voice just above a whisper.

"Well, of course, I'll help you. I certainly will." Sonya stepped down into the room and walked over to Velma. The front of her skirt was still wet where she had tried to wash the coffee from it.

Velma's heart fell. *Sonya. So that's why*, she thought. The woman knew Sonya was coming and had to remove all evidence that she was helping her. Then Velma remembered the washcloth that lay on the floor beside her. She inched her body over to conceal it.

"What would you like, Madam?" Sonya asked mockingly. "I came home early just to attend to Madam's needs." She laughed then continued, "I see you did your work today. Very good. I'll have to think of another reward to give you." She looked about the floor. "Let me see. Where is your last reward? Or did you have it for breakfast since you weren't too hungry at dinner last night? Leftovers are always better the next day, I've heard." She began to laugh again.

Velma dropped her head onto her chest, and tears filled her eyes as she thought about her slaughtered cat. Sonya's eyes fell on the tray that held Geronimo's remains. Velma had pushed it as far as she could away from her into a corner.

"Oh, there he is," Sonya said. She turned back to Velma and smirked down on her. "Are you enjoying having Geronimo here with you, Madam?"

Velma looked at Sonya, and she envisioned her fate in the hands of this mad woman. *Can only death release me from this? No, I won't believe that*, she thought.

"I'm home early, because your boyfriend was so upset about you, he dumped coffee all over my clothes," Sonya continued.

Velma looked at her, questioningly. "I have no idea what you're talking about, Sonya."

"Oh, are you saying you don't know that Mr. Bradley Morris, our ingenious creative department head, is in love with you?"

"Bradley? In love with me? That's absurd."

"Oh, is it?" He's your kind. What's the matter? Don't you think he's good enough for you? Or have you placed yourself above your people now? Are you hung up on White men, or just their money?"

"Sonya—" Velma began.

"Or, maybe you and Bradley planned this whole thing," Sonya interrupted her. "Maybe this was a conspiracy between the two of you. Perhaps Morris was your pimp. Maybe he saw a lucrative thing and sent his prize whore out to snare it. To swindle my father's legal heirs out of his company."

"Sonya, I loved William."

"Shut up!" Sonya screamed. "Don't talk about my father! Do you hear me? You're not fit to speak his name!" She stood for a few moments, breathing hard, seething. Then she began to pace. "So you loved my father...?"

"Yes."

"Well, Bradley Morris would have been a safer choice for you." Sonya's voice was soft but angry and threatening.

"Bradley Morris hates me."

"Oh? Why do you think he hates you?"

"For the same reason you do, I imagine."

"Really? If he were in love with you, I guess he would be upset about you and my father. But I don't believe that's the case." Sonya paused for a moment, and then went on. "You should have stayed with the Black man, Velma. But, no, you had to go after a White one. But not just any White man. You made sure he was wealthy as well. And you didn't care that he had a family who loved and needed him. I'll bet you spent many nights scheming, like a black widow spider, weaving your web, and then plotting how you were going to lure your prey into it. And my father was right there, the perfect sucker. Gullible. Weak!" She hung her head and began to weep. "I hate you, Daddy. I hate you. I hate you for leaving me."

Sonya's pitiful sobs came from deep within her, her voice sounding, perhaps, like a little girl whose father had spanked her for the first time. Velma felt sorry for the creature before her. This was the daughter of the man she had loved with all her heart. And she had promised him, on his deathbed, that she would look after her. What was she to do?

In spite of what Sonya was doing to her, Velma could not stop her heart from going out to this confused young woman.

"Sonya," she said softly.

Sonya's weeping stopped as quickly as it had begun, and she lashed out at Velma. "Shut up!" She raised her hand to strike Velma. Velma flinched. Sonya thought better of what she was about to do and lowered her hand. She began to pace, seething.

There's no reasoning with her, Velma thought. *She's beyond*—

"I followed you and my father many times," Sonya said, interrupting Velma's thoughts. "I would sit out in front of your building and wait for the two of you to come out. Especially on Saturday nights. You always went out on Saturday nights. Mostly to the Pier Marquee." She stopped and looked at Velma for a moment. "Was that your favorite restaurant, Velma?"

"Yes." Velma's voice was barely above a whisper.

"I thought it must have been, because he took you there so often. I would sit in my car and watch you walk inside, arm in arm," Sonya said. Then her voice changed, all the bitterness and hatred spilling over once again. "I was still there hours later when you came out, your arms about each other, stopping along the way sometimes to kiss and hold each other—like two teenagers experiencing love for the first time." She looked at Velma, her voice soft again. "I never saw him look at my mother the way he looked at you. Never. It was as if he saved all of that for you."

Sonya grew silent, tears welling in her eyes again. She cleared her throat and shook her head as if to clear it. "I guess I was living in a fairyland, Velma. Where everything was the way it should be. Family being the most important thing in a man's life."

"Sonya!" Harry called from the other room.

Sonya turned abruptly from Velma and went into Harry's room. She smiled sweetly at her other captive.

"Yes, Harry, what can I do for you?"

"Please, Sonya. Bring me something to eat. I'm so hungry."

"So am I. I'm going out to dinner in another hour or so. I shall bring your dinner when I return." She turned and started from the room.

"Not that damned piece of bread and water! You bring me some food, Sonya! Do you hear me?" he shouted at her retreating back.

Sonya went on out the door and closed it behind her.

"Sonya! Sonya!" Harry called, his voice frantic.

Sonya went past Velma and spoke as if she were saying goodbye to an old friend, "See you later."

She went up the stairs. The lights went out, and then the occupants in the basement heard the door at the top of the stairs slam.

Tom Simms left his old office. His arms were loaded down with his desk accessories: a solid oak frame quartz movement clock, four brass sculptures with onyx bases, framed pictures of his wife and children, a brass business card holder, and an oak double pen holder.

If he could not move his furniture into his new office (there was no doubt in his mind that Velma's office would soon be his) yet, he could at least look at his own accessories. He detested all the feminine gadgets that stared at him from atop Velma's desk. The desk itself was enough to make him look like a fool.

Well, it shouldn't be long before I'll be able to move in lock stock and barrel, he thought.

He had heard about the blood the police found in Velma's apartment. The woman had done a terrible thing to the Colby family. Maybe she was now reaping, atoning for her sins. Whatever, if Tom Simms could gain from it, so be it.

Tom went down the hallway to Velma's office. He laid his armload of valuables on the sofa. Then he walked over to the closet, opened it, removed all of the woman's pretty little trinkets from her desk, and threw them inside. He closed the closet door, walked back over to the sofa, and gently picked up his desk accessories.

"Life is wonderful," he whispered to himself. He began to hum as he arranged his treasures on top of the desk.

CHAPTER 28

Velma had been listening to the man in the next room cry for an awfully long time it seemed. She had not heard a man cry so pitifully since the day her mother was buried. She thought her father would gladly have climbed into the grave with his wife and been perfectly content. To this day, he had never gotten over his wife's death.

"If she had been sick, I could understand," he said. "But a heart attack...? It was just too sudden."

He had been devastated. They both had. But Velma had to be strong for her father. She had not grieved until much later, and it had been hard. But she was a survivor.

Her father had never married again, never even dated another woman. He just kept himself busy in the church: preaching the word, visiting the sick, and burying the dead. Velma worried about him, but he always assured her that he and the Lord were doing just fine. Whenever she went home to see him, that appeared to be true. He and the Lord seemed to have been doing just fine.

Velma could not help but smile. She had seen so many of her father's traits in William Colby. She wondered what those two men would have thought of each other if they had met.

And then, her thoughts were full of the two men who would always have a special place in her heart. One was lost to her forever. The other... she would have to go see him soon. And she would.

They always talked on Sundays. He told her about the service that morning at his church and always asked if she had gone to church. She had not been for a while now. Maybe...No, she would not allow any negative thoughts to enter her head. She had to stay positive.

She had not called him this past Sunday, and he had not gotten through to her, if he had called her, because her ordeal in Sonya's basement had already begun. Being the intuitive person that he was, and with his one-on-one relationship with God—"He talks to me, and I talk to him," he always told her—would he sense that something was wrong if he had left a message on her phone, and she had not returned his call? Would he come looking for her? Would he call the police and have them look for her?

"Please, God, let my father know that I'm in trouble," she prayed.

Somebody had to help her. As dire as this situation seemed, she would not allow herself to believe that her life would end like this. It could not.

She had been so consumed with the company lately, her personal life had become about nil. But she had a few friends outside the company, and they would be calling.

Somebody... Somebody.

The same God that had kept her father sane after her mother's death knew the predicament she was in now.

"Ask and it shall be given you...," she whispered.

Velma bowed her head and began to pray.

"Harry!" Velma called to the man in the other room a few minutes later. She heard the crying stop abruptly.

"What do you want?" came his reply after a moment.

"Crying is not going to help you, and neither is pleading with Sonya."

"Just shut up, woman! Just shut your damn mouth!"

"The next time Callie comes down here, I'm going to try to talk her into untying you," Velma continued as if she had not heard his outburst. "You're going to have to help me convince her that she should help you, too. Can't you remember some happy times the two of you shared here? A Christmas party or something else that brought the two of you together in a friendly atmosphere? If you could make her remember something, she might relate to you."

"I don't know. I can't think of anytime we've ever liked each other."

The man was impossible.

"You didn't have to like each other, Harry. Just a time when you had fun together."

A few moments passed, then he spoke, "Well, we did have fun at the parties sometime."

"Good. Think of some incident that everyone at one of the parties enjoyed. Something Callie is bound to remember."

"I can't think of anything," he said after a few moments.

"Then think of something Callie did that was amusing or smart. People love to have other people make a fuss over them."

"Callie Foster was never smart or amusing," he said, his voice sarcastic.

"No wonder she hates your guts, Harry," Velma snapped. "No wonder she finds it amusing seeing you in the defenseless position in which you are now. I can understand why she chooses to let you stay that way."

"What can I say? I was just being truthful."

"There's always some good in everyone, Harry. There might even be a spark somewhere in some deep, dark, recess in you!"

"Lady, you've got a real sharp tongue, you know that?"

What's the use? Velma thought. Just let him rot. But she didn't want to rot with him.

Velma heard the door at the top of the stairs open, almost simultaneously with the click of the light switch. Then she heard the sound of footsteps on the stairs.

In a few moments, Sonya glided into the room. "I'm back from dinner," she said cheerily.

She was stunning in a pale blue silk suit. A take out bag dangled in her hand. She walked over to Velma and stood, smiling down on her.

"I brought you a present just like I promised," she said sweetly.

Velma did not know what to expect. Had Sonya really brought her some food? Did she dare even hope? Even her leftovers would be welcomed.

Sonya turned the bag upside down, opened it, and dumped a white rat on Velma's head. The rat squeaked. Velma screamed, her arms flailing about her head. The rat scrambled down Velma's back then ran off into another part of the basement.

Sonya doubled over with laughter.

Velma finally spoke. She made a great effort to be as calm as possible. "Sonya, have you thought about what you're doing? You have to let Harry and me go. Kidnapping is a serious offense."

Sonya leered down on Velma. Her eyes blazed. Her gaiety was gone as quickly as it had come. "Yes, it is, isn't it? Why didn't you think about that when you kidnapped my father away from my mother and me!"

"I didn't—" Velma began.

"Yes, you did!" Sonya hit Velma upside the head with her fist. "You took him!" She began to pace, her eyes darting wildly about in her head. "You held him captive," she continued. "Bound with invisible chains, perhaps, but bound just the same. Do you deny it, Velma? Do you?"

Velma did not answer.

"You can't, can you?" Sonya began to weep, her voice soft, pitiful. "He never came back. But I kept hoping. I even prayed. I begged God to bring my father back to me. I told Him that Mother and I needed him." She paused. Her tears stopped, and her face became hard. She continued, her voice bitter, angry. "We needed my father!"

"Sonya, you had your father's love."

"But God didn't answer my prayers," Sonya continued as if Velma had not spoken. "He let you keep him. I watched my mother grovel, demean herself. She went to his grave constantly taking flowers. Then she took that last red rose, and that night," her voice, barely above a whisper now, "that night, she cut her throat." She began to sob again. "My mother cut her own throat because you took everything she had to live for away from her. My father was her whole life. After he left, she died a little each day. Then when he died, she... she... she couldn't live anymore. She didn't want to live for me." Uncontrollable sobs began to shake her body.

After a moment, she continued. "I don't have anyone anymore. I don't even have the company. He always told me, 'this is going to be all yours someday, Baby Girl.' Baby Girl. That's what he called me before...before he left us. He said I was his sweet, little baby girl."

Sonya wrapped her arms about herself and began to moan, rocking her body to and fro.

"Sonya, I'm so sorry."

"He said the company was going to be mine!" Sonya screamed. "That's what he said. He promised. And I believed my daddy. Then you took it away. You took everything away from me!"

Velma looked at the pitiful creature before her, and she thought about what the scriptures said about forgiveness. She knew she had to forgive this young woman, because she surely did not know what she was doing.

Velma remembered what her father had taught her when she was a little girl.

"Remember," he would say, "there's no problem so great that the Lord can't solve it, no predicament so dire that He can't deliver you from it. All you have to do is ask and believe."

"I believe," Velma whispered to herself.

Velma knew that intervention from a higher power was her only salvation from her present predicament. She began to pray for herself, for Sonya, and for Harry.

CHAPTER 29

Bradley parked his car a half block from the Colby estate and walked back to the house. He looked up at the oversized structure, that he was seeing for the first time, and whistled softly. Yes, he and William Colby had been buddies of sort at work, but the man had never invited him to his house. *What a monstrosity*, he thought. Looming like some sinister beast in the night. "Why do rich people have to always have everything so big?" he asked himself. He wondered if, when he became rich—and he was working on it—that question would still occupy a place in his mind.

Bradley walked stealthily to the front door of the house, the duplicate keys dangling in his hand. He had planned to come the next day, while Sonya was at the office, but he had not been able to fight the urgency within him. He knew that Velma was in danger, if not already dead, and that every second counted. Whatever clues he might find here at the Colby estate, he would find tonight. Tomorrow, he would be just that much closer to—whatever.

Bradley thought he would wait awhile before going inside. *Give Sonya time to fall into a deep sleep,* he thought.

He surveyed the situation about him. Plenty of shrubbery to leap into if someone was to come up to the house. And no alarm signs posted.

He crouched down beside the door to wait.

Sonya still stood weeping, rocking her body to-and-fro. "Why did you do it?"

"We loved each other."

"But why would he love you and not my mother? She was his wife," Sonya said, sounding like a confused child.

"He had loved your mother, Sonya, but things change. Times change, and we must live with the times. His time for loving your mother had ended." Velma's voice was soft and caring.

"And his time for loving you had begun?"

"Yes."

"And what about me? Didn't I matter?"

"Of course, you mattered, Sonya. Your father loved you very much."

"Then why didn't he stay with me? He knew how much I needed him. I needed my father."

"He was starting a new life with the woman he loved at that time."

"You."

"Yes, I was that woman."

"Did you know that you were sinning with my father, Velma?"

"It wasn't like you think, Sonya. We—" Velma began.

"Thou shalt not commit adultery!" Sonya snapped, interrupting Velma. "That's one of the things I learned at my church. Didn't they teach you that in yours? Did you go to church, Velma?"

"Yes, I still do. My father is a minister."

Sonya looked at her. She was shocked. "A minister? Your father is a minister?"

"Yes."

"Well, what kind of minister's daughter are you? How could you do the things you did, and pass yourself off as a minister's daughter? How could you?"

"Sonya, I—" Velma began.

"I used to go to church with my mother and father when I was a little girl," Sonya said, interrupting Velma again. Her voice was calm now. "We were happy then. Before you. We went to the Methodist Church. We even visited one of your people's churches, the African Methodist Episcopal Church. My father made sure I knew how to pronounce the name just right. My father was a good Christian, and he wanted to prove it by worshiping with everybody. We would read the Doxology with them. And there it was, 'Thou shalt not commit adultery.' The preacher would say it, and then we would sing, asking the Lord to have mercy and help us keep His laws." Her eyes met Velma's, searching for answers. "You didn't keep the law, Velma. Didn't you fear God?"

"Sonya, your father and I—" Velma began.

"No. No, you didn't keep the law, Velma!" Sonya screamed. "You sinned! You and my father broke God's law!"

She stopped for a moment then dropped her head. When she spoke again, her voice was calm. "And so did I. I sinned, too, Velma. I was weak then. But I don't have time for that now. I have to prove myself to my father. I have to make him see that I can run the company just as well as the son I might have been. He wanted a son when I was born. He told me that once. But he said he still loved me, and I believed him."

"He did love you, Sonya."

"I have to show him." Sonya stopped and looked absently about for a moment. "But, I can't now, can I? Because he's dead. He's dead, isn't he, Velma?"

"Yes," Velma said, her voice barely above a whisper.

"I remember when we buried him. The way she cried over his casket... She just couldn't stop crying. I wanted to take her in my arms and tell her everything was going to be all right. But I couldn't. After all he had done to us, she just kept on loving him, and I hated her for it." She stopped and looked sternly at Velma. "He was with you when he died. He should have been with his family, you know. And what were my mother and I supposed to do while he was starting a new life with you?"

"He wanted to maintain a good father-daughter relationship with you, Sonya. He tried so hard, but you wouldn't allow it."

"Because I couldn't forgive him for what he did to us. Can't you see that?"

"You could have at least tried to understand."

"Understand? How could I understand that my mother was wasting away, grieving over my father as if he were already in the grave? There were times when I wished he had been. It would have been easier. And what about my mother, Velma? My mother. What was she supposed to do?"

Velma had no answer.

"Was she supposed to pick up the pieces and go on with her life? Is that what you and my father expected her to do?" Sonya waited a moment then continued. "Well, what about her heart, Velma? He broke her heart. What was my mother going to do about her broken heart?" Sonya paused for a moment then screamed, her face becoming instantly distorted with rage. "He destroyed her!" Her fist shot out and caught Velma upside the head.

"No! Sonya!" Velma screamed.

"Hey! What's going on out there?" Harry yelled from the other room.

Velma threw up her hands trying to ward off the blows that continued to both sides of her head. Sonya finally stopped hitting her. Velma watched as the younger woman sank to the floor, her eyes glued to the enemy, watching, on guard.

After a few moments, Sonya got up, her eyes still fixed on Velma's face.

For a while, Velma thought she might be able to get through to the younger woman. But now... Now she knew Sonya was completely beyond reasoning.

Sonya began to cry again, the tears coursing, unchecked, down her face. "It's easy for you to talk. You were happy. You had what we wanted more than anything else in the world. You had my father, my mother's husband,

and we had nothing." She began to moan, rocking her body to-and-fro, her gaze still on the enemy.

Then Velma saw her. Callie was sneaking down the stairs, a poker held high above her head. She moved stealthily up behind Sonya. Velma watched as the poker came down on the back of Sonya's head. Sonya fell to the floor and lay still, her eyes closed.

Callie laughed—a wild, shrieking sound. She dropped the poker and ran to Velma. She pulled a key from her pocket and started to fumble with the manacles about Velma's wrists.

"Oh, thank God," Velma cried. "Hurry, Callie. Hurry."

"What's going on out there? What's happening?" Harry yelled from the other room.

After a number of futile attempts, Callie freed Velma's hands. Velma took the key and unlocked the chains that bound her ankles.

"Hey, out there! What's going on?" Harry yelled again.

Velma attempted to rise but fell back to the floor, her body aching, paining, too weak to maneuver the move on its own. Callie helped her get to her feet, and they moved, slowly at first, across the floor, Velma pulling toward the room where Harry was being held and Callie toward the basement stairs.

"We have to help him, too, Callie. We have to untie Harry."

Callie did not seem to hear. She yanked at Velma's arm until Velma gave in and moved along with her toward the stairs. They started up them, Velma willing her legs to move.

"Hey, out there! Hey!" Harry yelled again.

Sonya stirred. She lay still for a moment then stirred again. She sat up, felt the back of her head, closed her eyes momentarily then looked about for her victim.

"No!" she screamed as she spotted the loose chains on the floor. She leaped to her feet, turned, and saw the women on the stairs. She raced after them.

Velma and Callie were near the top of the stairs when Velma heard Sonya scream. She looked back to see Sonya bolting up the stairs behind them. Velma shoved Callie out in front of her into the back hallway then followed as swiftly as she could, slamming the door behind her. She was about to lock it when Sonya crashed through it, knocking Velma to the floor.

Sonya's eyes fell on Callie who was running down the hallway. She took off after her, overtook her, and the two women began to struggle.

Velma picked herself up off the floor and looked about for a weapon. She saw nothing. She finally unfastened her belt and yanked it from about her waist.

Sonya threw Callie to the floor, straddled her, and began to choke her. Velma ran up behind Sonya and threw the belt around Sonya's neck. She pulled, and Sonya fell backward, releasing her hold on Callie. Sonya flipped over, grabbed Velma's ankles and pulled. Velma hit the floor.

Callie got groggily up from the floor, holding her throat and coughing, her eyes glued to the wrestling women on the floor. She had to help the woman, save her from that crazy girl.

Callie had known the girl was crazy the day the brazen, little hussy sashayed back into the house and took over—after being gone for years. Callie had been forced to take refuge in the servants' quarters, hiding out, never going into other parts of the house until after the girl left during the day, or after she went to bed at night. Then she would go up to her bedroom, take a nice, long bath and change her clothes.

Callie had heard about crazy people, the terrible things they did. And this girl was totally mad. Callie had seen it in her eyes. She had watched the girl from the upstairs hallway the first day she came back—the way her eyes darted about in her head, the way she had stormed through the house, screaming at the top of her voice about "settling the score." Was it any wonder that Callie feared for her life? That's why she hid downstairs. She knew the girl would never come into that part of the house.

But the night the other woman had come, she had sneaked out of her hiding place to see who the girl's visitor was. Callie thought the woman looked familiar, that she had seen her somewhere before, but she could not remember where.

Callie had seen everything that night. She had watched the girl put something in the woman's drink. She had seen her beat the woman then drag her downstairs and chain her. She had seen the girl put the key to the chains in a cabinet in the kitchen then lock it. Tonight, she had found Sonya's keys on the kitchen counter. She had unlocked the cabinet, gotten the key to the chains, and set the woman free.

She had thoroughly enjoyed the way the girl had tricked Harry the night he was captured. Yes, the girl was smart. And now that the girl knew she was still in the house, Callie had to make her next move. But she did not want to leave the house. It should really be hers now. After all, she was the one who stayed with it—had been imprisoned in it for years. She was the one who took care of it. *I'd like to chase that little heifer right out that front door*, she thought.

But first things first.

Callie noticed that the woman was losing ground with that crazy girl. She had to help the woman get free.

Callie kicked off her high-heeled shoes, picked up one of them, and, after a few moments of waiting for the right opportunity, hit Sonya over the head with it. Sonya, dazed for a moment, fell off Velma to the floor. Velma struggled to her feet. Callie grabbed her by the arm and pulled her into the living room.

"Let's get out of here, so we can get help," Velma said, starting for the front door.

Callie shook her head. "No key." She pulled Velma toward the stairs.

Velma finally gave up trying to make it to the door and followed Callie up the stairs to the second floor.

Sonya came through the hall door into the living room and bounded up the stairs behind the other women. She grabbed Velma by the ankle just as Velma and Callie reached the top of the stairs. Velma fell. Sonya fell on top of her, and they began to tussle.

Callie, confused, turned round and round observing the two women fighting at the top of the stairs. She finally grabbed Sonya by the hair and pulled her off Velma. She hit Sonya on the back of the head with her fist, and Sonya fell forward to the floor. Callie leaped onto Sonya's back, grabbed her by the hair, and began jerking her head up and down, smashing Sonya's face on the floor. Sonya finally managed to throw Callie off her back and scrambled to her feet. She ran toward Velma who was just getting to her feet. Velma braced herself for battle. They fought.

Callie leaped up, raced over to the women, and grabbed Sonya from behind, her right arm slipping around Sonya's neck in a chokehold. She dragged Sonya a few feet before Sonya broke loose, flinging Callie across the room. Callie landed on her back. Sonya leaped for her, sailing through the air as if she had suddenly sprouted wings. Callie's feet came up and caught Sonya in the midriff, sending her stumbling back across the floor. She landed on her back. Callie got up and leaped for Sonya. Sonya rolled out of the way, and Callie hit the floor.

The two women leaped to their feet about the same time and began to stalk each other—circling, their eyes wild, fastened on each other's face. All of a sudden, as if on cue, they charged and clashed. They fought fiercely, wildly, like the two insane women they were. After a few moments, Sonya overpowered Callie, dragged her over to the banister, and hoisted her up onto it. Callie's body hung ominously over the railing.

"No! Stop, Sonya! Stop!" Velma screamed. *She's going to kill her*, she thought. She pulled herself up off the floor and tried to run over to the women. She grimaced in pain and fell back to the floor. "My ankle," she moaned.

Callie looked down and saw her plight. She screamed.

Bradley bolted upright upon hearing screams from inside the house. He began to try the keys in the lock on the door. In a few moments, he found the right one and opened the door just in time to see the woman fall over the banister and crash to the floor below.

"Velma!" he shouted.

"Bradley," Velma whispered. "Thank God."

Bradley raced over to Callie who lay sprawled on the living room floor below the second floor banister.

"Bradley! Up here!" Velma cried.

Bradley turned his gaze to the upstairs hallway just as Sonya grabbed Velma around the neck and began dragging her over to the banister.

Bradley took the stairs three at a time. "Sonya!" he shouted as he leaped onto the upstairs hallway.

Sonya released her hold on Velma letting her fall to the floor. Then she turned and snarled at Bradley, her eyes wild. She hissed at him like a wild cat then pounced on him, her legs wrapping about his waist—biting, scratching, and pummeling him about the head.

Bradley was surprised at the strength of the woman as he struggled against her. He whirled round and round trying to dislodge her hold on him. He soon realized that if he was going to win this battle, he had to give it all he had. Bradley grabbed Sonya's hair with his left hand and pulled her head back. His right fist shot out and caught her on the left jaw. Her legs went limp. She started to fall. Bradley held her up by her hair. His fist connected with her jaw once more. He gave that one everything he had. He released her, and she crumpled to the floor at his feet.

This time, she did not move.

Bradley and Velma simply looked at each other for a few moments. Then Bradley pulled his cell phone from his pocket and dialed 911.

Bradley finished his call then knelt beside Velma on the floor. He took her in his arms, holding her close, stroking her arms, her back, her neck, her face, her hair, as she let out all the pent-up emotions within her.

They stayed that way until they heard sirens outside the house.

Bradley reluctantly released Velma and hurried down the stairs. He had not wanted to let her go. He just wanted to hold her, protect her. He did not fully understand those feelings.

The knot in his stomach was tighter than it had ever been.

CHAPTER 30

The four ambulances careened into the emergency driveway of the Baltonville Memorial Hospital. Out of the first and second ambulances came Callie and Velma. They were rushed into emergency. Bradley, who had talked the attendants into letting him ride in the back of the second ambulance with Velma, was in close pursuit. Harry walked out of the third ambulance. He had refused to get on the stretcher, saying he did not need medical attention. He just wanted to go home.

"After we get your statement down, sir," one of the policemen said.

Out of the fourth ambulance jumped Sonya. She took off running back down the driveway from which the ambulance motorcade had come. Two attendants were hot on her heels. She had surprised them, just as the doors opened, by leaping off the stretcher, toppling all of the equipment, and knocking the stunned men out of her way as she raced from the opening.

The driver stood looking on in wide-eyed amazement for a few moments, then he decided he had better join in the chase.

"This chick can run," the first man yelled over his shoulder to the man running behind him as he huffed and puffed trying to catch up with Sonya.

"Show her what you're made of," the second man said. He was just about as winded as the first.

"Likewise," the first man shot back.

The first man caught up with Sonya and grabbed her from behind. She whirled around and growled, clawing at his face with both hands. He screamed and stopped in his tracks, holding his injured face.

The second man had reached them by this time. He grabbed Sonya, and she bit him on the hand. He yelled, released her, and stood for an uncertain moment looking at his hand.

Sonya was off again.

The driver, an apparent slow runner, still had not caught up with them. The first and second men took up the chase again.

"Holy Moses!" one yelled.

"She's out of her skull," said the other man.

The first man caught up with her and leaped, tackling her from behind. They went down on the pavement, Sonya on her stomach, the man on his knees trying to hold her feet. Sonya flipped her body over and kicked the man in the groin. He fell forward, clutching himself and moaning. Sonya leaped to her feet.

The driver was finally on the scene, and before Sonya could take off again, his right fist shot out and caught her on the left side of her head. The second man caught her as she fell.

"That's the only way to handle cases of this sort," the driver said, blowing on his aching hand. He led the party back up the driveway to the hospital, Sonya swinging between the first and second men who had hauled her up by her wrists and ankles.

"She's a case for the nut house for sure," one of the men said.

Callie's neck had been broken in the fall she had taken over the banister, but, miraculously, she was expected to live. She was rushed straight into surgery. And, after a few phone calls and brief conversations at the Baltonville Police Department, the four-year old unsolved Colby jewelry theft case was reopened. They were sure they had finally

217

caught their thief, since some of the stolen Colby jewels were found around Callie's neck, on her fingers, and about her wrists.

Sonya was put in restraints then wheeled into the hospital. After a careful examination, she was hauled off to the state hospital for the criminally insane.

Velma, after emergency treatment, was admitted to the hospital. When she was settled in her room, the police began their interrogation.

Harry was treated and, after a brief interrogation by the police, released. "I'm getting out of this town while the getting is good," he said to himself as he hurried away from the hospital.

Bradley was questioned. Then, much to his dismay, he was not allowed to stay in Velma's room while the police questioned her. He was told to wait outside. He did, and the interrogation went on for hours, it seemed.

Bradley finally tired of trying to elude reporters in the corridors. He took a cab back to Sonya's house, got his car, and went home. But he did not sleep. His thoughts were too full of Velma Hannah (the woman he had told himself time and time again that he hated) and the horrifying events she had just gone through. He shuddered whenever he thought of what might have happened if he had not gotten into that house when he did. Velma Hannah would probably be dead.

What was wrong with him anyway? Why was he worrying so much about this particular woman? Was he losing his touch? But there was no denying his feelings whenever he saw her. When he had held her in his arms a few hours earlier... Bradley could not describe the feeling that had come over him. A feeling he had never experienced before in his life. Out of all the women who had marched in and out of his life, there wasn't one who had ever made him feel the way he did when he was near Velma Hannah.

"Is this what it feels like to be in love?" he asked himself out loud. *If it is, I don't know if I want it,* he thought. It was like some idiot had taken up residency in his body and he was powerless to stop him from acting like the idiot he was.

He could not control whatever was happening to him, and Bradley Morris was a man who was always in control, especially where women were concerned. He cringed, thinking about the titles he presently held: ladies' man, womanizer, playboy, et cetera—all blown to hell.

"Damn," he mumbled to himself.

Bradley was sure Velma hated him as much as he thought he hated her. Oh, he knew she was grateful to him for saving her from her impending fate, but to expect more would be a bit presumptuous, even for him.

What was he going to do?

Bradley wanted to call Velma just to talk. He wanted to get up out of the bed, in which he knew he would not get a moment's sleep that night, and go back to the hospital just to look at her.

He did neither. He merely stared into the darkness trying to will his mind to stop torturing him.

The next morning, Harry Reynolds was on a plane to Canada. He thought his story to the police the night before had been most convincing. He told them it was all a misunderstanding, and he didn't want to press charges against anybody. All he wanted to do was go home and get some rest. But as convincing as he thought it sounded, he did not want to be around if the police ever found out the truth about how he had ended up in the clutches of Sonya Colby. Velma Hannah could not tell them anything definite, but there was always the possibility that Sonya might someday rejoin the world of reality and tell them all.

Harry had known for a long time that his time had run out in Baltonville. He now realized he had been a fool to try to press it. He wondered what the future held for him in Canada.

He would soon find out.

CHAPTER 31

Bradley walked down the hospital corridor, a stern expression on his face. His steps were heavy, his stride even. Bradley was angry and with good reason. He held a crumpled newspaper in one hand. He reached the door to the room he wanted and shoved it open.

Velma looked up from her bed at the sound of the door opening. She was surrounded by flowers. They overran the bedside table and spilled onto the windowsill, then the floor. Most of them were from Bradley. Flower shops from all over Baltonville had been delivering them all morning. They were still coming in at intervals.

"What is this crap I'm reading?" Bradley blurted, throwing the paper on the bed beside Velma.

Velma smiled up at him. "Thanks for all the flowers."

"Forget the flowers! Why didn't you tell them the truth, woman? For God's sake?"

"She's sick, Bradley."

"She's also a criminal! She kidnapped you and tried to kill you. You and a few other people. Me included."

"Shhhhh, you're in a hospital," Velma said, a smile playing on her lips.

"Yeah, yeah." His sighed and shook his head.

"I went there of my own volition, Bradley."

"Well, you certainly didn't leave there of your own volition. You should have pressed charges."

"She's not competent to stand trial. You know that."

"Neither is that old woman, but they're slapping that theft charge on her head," he snapped. "She made the papers, too."

Velma's face clouded. "I know. I read the article. I'm going to do all I can to help her. I'll hire the best lawyers in the country to represent her if they take her to court." She looked up at Bradley, her voice a bit shaky. "If it hadn't been for her..." She left the sentence unfinished.

"You might not be here now." Bradley finished the sentence for her. "That woman saved your life."

"Yes, she did. She's a good person, and I have to help her. I owe it to her."

"All it takes is money, lady: the battery on which this country runs, and you've got it. Thanks to your *Bitter Inheritance*."

Velma sighed, her face grave. "Bradley I shouldn't have caused that family so much pain."

He looked at her and smiled wryly. "Loving and being loved is not wrong, Velma. You once chided me for talking to the man about the women in my life. Well, he talked to me about his wife. His marriage was over long before you came on the scene."

"I know, but she still loved him." Her voice was almost a whisper.

"That was not your problem."

"I know," she said, but her voice was not too convincing. She thought about Claire Colby on the night of William's death. How the woman had sobbed as if her heart would break—and it had, six months later when she took her own life. Velma closed her eyes as tears began to well up in them. She had never seen anyone in so much pain, and she was sorry for the part she had played in causing that pain.

"He was searching, and he found you," Bradley offered. "The man loved you. He wanted to marry you, not just play around with you. William Colby was a realist. He was a good man. I don't know why he had to die. I guess that just wasn't for you. But be a realist like he was. You're a rich woman now. Most African-American women don't have your kind of luck."

Velma's eyes darted to him, a scornful look on her face. "I don't consider having the man I loved die as being lucky, Bradley."

Bradley threw up his hands in a defeated gesture and backed off a step. "Don't misconstrue what I'm saying. Of course, I'm not saying you're a lucky woman because the man is dead. But in a sense, you are."

She glared at him, shaking her head. "That's an ambiguous statement if I've ever heard one."

"Just hear me out, will you? I'm just telling it like it is. Dealing with the facts as I see them. And the fact is, the man is dead. Be thankful for what your relationship with him and his death have given you. You did what you had to do to climb that ladder, and it paid off for you."

"What do you mean, I did what I had to do?"

Bradley hesitated a moment, then proceeded cautiously. "Velma, you have to know what everyone at the agency is saying about you."

"Tell me, Bradley, what is everyone saying?"

He looked at her for a moment, then blurted. "That you slept your way up the ladder and into the man's life. What else?"

"And is that what you believe?"

"I don't know what to believe," he said after a moment of deliberation.

"Of course, you believe it just like everybody else. Isn't that the way it's usually done? Women employees always hop in and out of bed with the powers-that-be in order to move up in the business world? Why should my situation be any different?"

"Because maybe you're different. I don't know," he said, his voice almost inaudible.

"We're all just a bunch of aspiring whores, right?" she continued, and then stopped, looked up at him, a confused look on her face. "What did you just say?"

His eyes held hers, his hand gently stroking her fingers. "There's just something about you. You're different."

"You're so right, Mr. Morris. I am different." She jerked her hand away from his. "You see, for your information, I am still a virgin."

The lump in Bradley's throat felt as if it was about to strangle him. He did not realize he was holding his breath until he experienced a strange sensation as if he were about to pass out. *Breathe, fool,* he thought. He gulped some air into his lungs. A virgin? He could not believe it. Not in this day and age. He had heard about a few here and there. But Velma?

Something about her told him that she was different. But a virgin? He looked at her, opened his mouth to speak, but nothing came out.

"Close your mouth," she said.

Bradley's mouth snapped shut.

"There are a few of us around, and the number is getting larger every day," she continued.

"I didn't...I thought...I, I..." he stammered.

"I know what you thought, what everybody else thought."

"No, I didn't. Well, maybe I did, but... I don't know."

"Just shut up," she snapped. "I did not sleep my way into my inheritance—which is more than I ever dreamed would come of my relationship with William Colby. I didn't have to do that, Bradley, because, you see, he loved me. He loved me enough to respect my wishes not to have sex until we were married. I loved him even more for that." She paused for a moment, and then laughed as she looked up into Bradley's ashen, confused face. "Sit down before you pass out."

Bradley obediently sat on a chair beside the bed.

"I didn't know what to think of the feelings I was having for the man at first, but as time passed, my admiration and respect for William Colby grew. I realized that I was fortunate, indeed, to be a part of a relationship where two people loved each other so much they defied all conviction, were ready to attempt to break down barriers, love their way through man-made obstacles."

She looked at Bradley, searching his eyes for a bit of understanding. *He's still as confused as ever*, she thought.

"Love encompasses the whole person, Bradley," she continued. "It's one of the most beautiful things that could ever happen to a man and a woman, and it doesn't always have to include the sex act."

"I, I know that," he stammered. "It's just that…" He was at a loss for words for a few moments. When he recovered, his next words caught Velma completely off guard. "But why him? Why a White man?" There, he had finally asked the question that had been on his mind for years. He had to know.

"Maybe because he understood me. And maybe he could understand where I was coming from because he was an older man, wiser than most."

"And no African-American man could have understood?"

"Oh, I'm sure eventually I would have found someone. William Colby just happened to come along before I got around to that brother whoever he might have been. Would you have understood, Bradley?"

Bradley sighed.

"If you and I had dated, would you have hung around after I refused your sexual advances a couple of times—or even once for that matter? If I had told you I was a virgin and planned to stay that way until I was married, would you have continued to see me?"

"I don't know," Bradley said.

"Oh, you know, Mr. Heart Throb, every woman's dream. Just snap your fingers, and watch the women come running," Velma threw up at him.

"Okay, so he was an exceptional man. I'll give him that. But that's past history. Let's get past it, shall we? The fact remains that you seem to still be grieving over the man."

"Maybe I am. William and I had something very special."

"That might be true, but you have your whole life before you and a huge responsibility that has been handed to you. And remember, no great dissertations or grieving on your part will bring the man back. Lastly, stop berating yourself over that girl. Take advantage of the situation at hand."

"I promised her father."

The muscles in Bradley's jaws tightened. He could feel the anger rising inside him. "Well, excuse me! I'm so tired of hearing about what he wanted. What do you want, lady? The man is six feet under. Wake up!" He whirled and started for the door.

"Don't go, Bradley."

Bradley stopped, his back still to her.

"I'm just trying to be fair," Velma continued. "He left me in charge of his agency, because he knew I would be fair to his daughter and do what was best for the agency."

He swung back around to face her. "What is best for the agency is not to involve that girl in anyway. I can tell you that."

"I know, but half the agency is still legally hers. If she's ever competent to return to the agency, or even to society, all I can do is be there for her. I can't just write her off when I promised her father, on his deathbed, that I would look after her as best I could. I guess my inheritance didn't come without a price."

"Did it ever cross your mind that William left you the agency not because he loved you so much, but because he had no choice in the matter?"

"What are you intimating now?" Velma asked, her voice impatient.

"I'm sure he did a lot of thinking before he penned his last will and testament," Bradley continued. "After all, who was going to continue his work if he should die? I believe he thought about that, lady. His wife knew nothing about the business. His daughter knew nothing about the business, and she was a teenager at that time. Tom Simms knows the business, but he's also a greedy fool. He certainly would not have worked for the betterment of the agency. He would have been only thinking of himself—whatever he could get out of it. Now you—William Colby knew he could trust you to carry on in the same manner in which he had. In my opinion, he had two choices, and you were the better of the two."

Bradley looked at her. He did not know what kind of reaction to expect from her. He had said what was on his mind. In all these years, he still had never learned how to "sit on it."

Much to his surprise, she was not angry. After a few moments of contemplation, she turned to him with a faraway look in her eyes.

"He loved me, Bradley. I don't doubt that for one second, but he also loved his company. He spent many hours training me. He wanted me to know everything. I thought it strange at first. Then I just fell into the habit. But, I swear, I had no idea what he had in mind."

"I believe you," Bradley said. "I also believe he made the right decision. I must commend you, lady. You didn't let him down. I'm ashamed to say that I was surprised at first, until I took a good look at you and your standards. Then I guess I was intimidated by your ability and jealous that the man had won your heart. I apologize for being such an ass."

Velma smiled up at him. "I guess I never took the time to get to know you either, Mr. Bradley Morris." Her voice began to tremble, and tears welled in her eyes. "If you hadn't—"

"It's all right," he said covering her hand with his own.

An awkward silence ensued for a few moments, and then Bradley removed his hand and looked at Velma, his wheels turning. "Look, I'm going to throw something at you, and you can take it for what it's worth." He paused for a moment as if collecting his thoughts.

"I'm listening," Velma said.

"Maybe…just maybe the best thing you could do for Sonya would be to get out of her life. Give up the agency. Sell it, take your half of the money and—"

"Run?" she said, finishing the sentence for him. "That's not my style, Bradley. I won't give up my company. All I've worked for all these years."

"You didn't let me finish," Bradley said. "You could start your own agency. It would be yours: The Velma Hannah Agency, if you will. As part owner of The William E. Colby Agency, you would always be beholden to William Colby and his daughter. I agree that she's the one with the problem, but it will also be your problem as long as you stay there. You're in a position to call the shots in your own life. You don't have to answer to anyone. Break away from your dead past. You have your escape if you want it."

"Never." Velma's voice was stern.

"I'll go with you. You would have the best creative department in the land, anyway."

Velma could not help but chuckle. "You're a man of true humility, Mr. Morris."

"Just a suggestion. Trust me. Whatever you decide, I'm with you. Remember that."

"Thank you. I appreciate it."

"All I'm asking you to do is think about it. Maybe Sonya's lawyer could arrange to buy you out of the agency."

"He'd like nothing better," she said, a wry smile playing on her lips. "But my answer is no."

"Okay. We'll do it your way."

"Bradley?" she said softly.

"Yes?"

"I can never thank you enough."

"No thanks necessary, lady."

He's nicer than I imagined, she thought. *He can be so brass and crude at times and yet so gentle. He's not much of a businessman though. If I'm going to end up with this man, I'm going to have to train him.*

"Now let me tell you something," she began, her eyes boring into his. "I know I could start my own company, and, in a few years, it would probably be thriving. But why should I when I've been given one that is already established? I'm not going to try to sell my company or leave it in the hands of a deranged person and a greedy, conniving snake like Tom Simms. I appreciate your concern for me and for the agency, but I know that next to William Colby, I am the best thing that ever happened to that company. I know it from ground up. It's in my blood now, a part of me, and I will never give it up—not even for Sonya's sake. I feel sorry for her, but I'm no fool."

"Go on. I'm listening," Bradley said.

"Bradley, I've always wanted to be my own boss. My father always taught me that was the way to go. I knew someday I was going to make it, but even in my wildest dreams, I never thought I would be in control of a multimillion-dollar company this early in my life. And now that I am, I'm going to stay there. I deserve it. I don't know why it happened, and I'm not going to question it. But I am going to make it work for me. This inheritance is going to take me where I'm supposed to be in life." She chuckled. "They hate us so much, Bradley, and what have we ever done to them?"

"What, indeed?"

"We slaved for them, made them rich while we had nothing. Most of us still have nothing. Well, that has changed for me, and one of them brought about that change in my life. I'm a rich woman now, and I'm not going to just hand my newfound wealth back over to the enemy. I loved William Colby, and he loved me. When things began developing with that man, I was thankful that if it had to happen, at least it was with a rich one."

Bradley began to clap his hands as if applauding a great performance, and then he laughed. "Good move."

"Make fun of me if you want," she said, chuckling in spite of herself. Then she continued. "Whether it was out of his love for me or his love for the agency, he entrusted his most valued possession to me, and I'm going to run it with or without his daughter. If, or when, she comes back, I'm going to try to make things as easy for her as possible—and try to be a friend. That's what her father wanted."

"Shall we pray for a miracle?" he said, bowing his head.

She laughed. "You're impossible." Her face became serious again. "As we grow older, we do grow wiser. Life is too short."

"Amen."

"I owe it to William. I promised."

"I know, and your word is your bond."

"That's right. I also owe it to our clients to stay with the agency. They need the business, and the business needs me. As soon as I'm released from this place, I'm going back where I belong, where William Ellis Colby put me. That's my decision, Mr. Morris. Are you still with me?"

"All the way. I'll be whatever you want me to be."

He reached down and took her hand in his. He felt his heart leap, and his insides churn. "So you loved him?"

"Yes, I did."

"Had you ever been in love before?"

"Yes, a couple of times at least. How about you?" She raised a skeptical eyebrow.

"I thought I was a few times, but right now, I'm not so sure, and I have you to thank for this befuddlement in my brain."

"Me?"

He raised her hand to his lips and kissed it, letting it linger there for a moment. He gave her back her hand, and a few moments of silence passed between them. She knew he wanted to kiss her lips, and, for some strange reason, she wanted him to do so.

"I had an ulterior motive for saving your life," Bradley offered.

"Is that right?"

Should he tell her how he really felt? Suppose she laughed in his face. Suppose she... The hell with it. As she said, life was too short. He had never bared his soul to any woman, but if he didn't tell this woman how he felt about her, he was going to burst.

Here goes everything, or nothing, he thought.

"Velma, I've got to tell you something. I wanted to wait until you got out of here, but I can't. I've got to get it out—now."

She looked at him, concerned. "What is it?"

"Okay. I know you've heard things about me and women. But, as I said earlier, that's in the past. I don't know whether I'm going or coming anymore. Whenever I look at you, my insides go crazy. My dreams are full of you, lady. Night and day, you're on my mind. As the old saying goes: 'I eat, sleep and drink you.' And this has been going on ever since the first day I laid eyes on you. When the thought occurred to me that you might be dead, I swear, my heart stopped. Every time I spoke your name, my voice choked in my throat. When I heard you calling to me at the Colby house... Just the sound of your voice—"

Her laughter stopped him in mid sentence.

She's laughing at me. She thinks I'm a stone fool, he thought. So much for baring his soul. Then he saw tears forming in her eyes. She wasn't laughing anymore, just looking at him with those incredibly beautiful eyes.

He didn't know what to think, but he had come this far. He bravely went on. "I've never even kissed you, but I know without a doubt that I love you, lady."

This man is saying all the right things, Velma thought. Did she dare hope? What was she feeling for him? She wasn't sure, but for some reason, having him around seemed so right. When he held her in his arms at the Colby estate, she not only felt safe but as if she belonged there.

She shook her head. What was she thinking? Bradley Morris? Could he really be the man she had been waiting for all of her adult life?

Then she heard her father's voice just as plainly, as if he were in the room with her, "Doubt is a major blessing blocker."

A tear rolled down the side of her face. Bradley wiped it away with a finger.

"You know, marriage never crossed my mind before, but I can't seem to think of anything else anymore. You and it just seem to go together," he said. "Why don't we go to dinner when you get out of here… and talk?"

A few more tears escaped her eyes, and he wiped them away.

"You can give me your answer later. When you're feeling better. I'll be back this evening if Mr. Simms hasn't fired me for taking off in the middle of the morning. Then, if he has, I'll be right back."

"I still do the hiring and firing at The William E. Colby Agency," Velma said.

"Yes, boss lady."

"That's right."

"You get some rest, and watch the watered down details of your ordeal on television." He bent down and kissed her forehead then turned to leave. "See you, baby," he said. Then, realizing what he had said, he turned back around, a smirk playing on his lips. "I mean, Miss Hannah."

"How about Velma?"

"How about Vel?"

"Not at the office."

"Deal." He pinched her cheek. "There might be hope for you yet." He turned to leave then whirled back around. "Oh, yes!" he exclaimed. "I had personnel call your father this morning. He was already on his way. He should be here shortly."

Velma produced a big smile. "Oh, I knew my daddy would be looking for me."

"I guess that makes two of us who would do anything to make sure you're safe."

A moment of silence passed between them as they looked into each other's eyes.

"Thanks, Bradley," Velma finally said, her voice barely above a whisper, her eyes brimming with tears.

"You're welcome." He saluted her, then turned and left the room.

She smiled as she looked after him.

A virgin. I'm not sure I can handle this, Bradley thought, as he strolled down the hospital corridor. He looked heavenward and whispered, "Lord, give me strength."

THE END

Some comments about *Bitter Inheritance*

"This was a book I was not able to put down. I was driven to find out how bitter someone driven by hatred could be. Kept me in suspense." R. Cooley, Producer/Filmmaker, Chicago.

"A real page-turner. Can't wait to see the movie," Megan Willingham, Radio Talk Show Host, California.

Other Reader Comments

"I could not put this book down. Fantastic read!"

"Keeps your interest from opening to cliff-hanging end."

"A fanciful feast for the senses."

"I was so into this book, I could not put it down. I was even reading the book while stopped at red lights. I went to Vegas, and I could not wait to get back to the room to read."

"Wonderful! Could not put it down. Read it in two evenings after working all day. Loved the fight scene."

"Thoroughly enjoyed. This lady can weave a story."

"It was painful reading at times, but I had to finish it, because it was so good."

"Did not want to stop reading to do anything else. Fantastic."

"This book is profoundly entertaining. Look out, you other writers. This writer is the craftswoman of psychological novels centered on murder!"

"Gripping and suspenseful. You can't wait to turn the page."

"What great writing. Callie is off the hook."

"Fantastic! The female James Patterson."

"Need to escape for a while? This book will take you on an adventure you will never forget."

The Making
Of
Bitter Inheritance, the Movie
2011

Starring

MILLENA GAY
HOWARD HEWETT
MARLA GIBBS
PHILLIP McCANN
TOM S. FOLEY
BARBARA GANNEN
MICHAEL COLYAR
KATHLEEN BRADLEY
HEATHER S. MICHAELS
PATRICKA D'ARBO
STONEY JACKSON
SHYLA LaSHA
JACEE JULE
TROY WILLIAMS

Directed by:
ANGELA GIBBS
Musical Score by:
Grammy Award Winner, HOWARD HEWETT
Assisted by: MATILDA HAYWARD and AMIL GIBBS
Script Adaptation by:
MILDRED DUMAS, FRANK UNDERWOOD, JR.
ALONZO AND AQUA JONES
Executive Producer:
MILLENA GAY
Produced by:
FRANK UNDERWOOD, JR. and LARRY KIRKLEY
Graphics and Web Design by:
LARRY KIRKLEY

www.ingramcontent.com/pod-product-compliance
Lightning Source LLC
Chambersburg PA
CBHW021240260626
47155CB00004BA/1243